THE HOLY SPIRIT IN THE THIRD MILLENNIUM

A Handbook on the Holy Spirit:
A Guide to the Spirit Within

Stanford E. Linzey, Jr.

Copyright © 2003 by Stanford E. Linzey, Jr.

The Holy Spirit in the Third Millennium
by Stanford E. Linzey, Jr.

Printed in the United States of America

Library of Congress Control Number: 2002117707
ISBN 1-591604-37-0

All rights reserved. No part of this publication may be reproduced or transmitted in any form or by any means without written permission of the publisher.

Unless otherwise indicated, Bible quotations are taken from the New International Version. Copyright © 1984 by Zondervan Publishing House.

Xulon Press
10640 Main Street
Suite 204
Fairfax, VA 22030
(703) 934-4411
XulonPress.com

To order additional copies, call 1-866-909-BOOK (2665).

for

Darnelle

Comments About
The Holy Spirit in the Third Millennium

"This book will touch you to the roots of your being. You won't put this book down. You are about to be blessed."
Oral Roberts, Founder/Chancellor
Oral Roberts University

"Carefully documented and solidly referenced in the New Testament. Relevant and meaningful. Strongly recommended."
Ben Armstrong, Ph.D.
Former Executive Director
National Religious Broadcasters

"A definitive work on the Holy Spirit. Personal experiences add to the appeal and verification."
Ronny Svenhard, National President
Business Men's Fellowship U.S.A.

"The inspired voice of Dr. Stanford Linzey rises through the cacophony of our times and speaks forth on the activity and methods of the Holy Spirit. New ways of the Holy Spirit are the old ways released into a fresh generation of inspired Christians."
Rev. David A. Womack
Former Managing Editor
The Gospel Publishing House

"Terrific! Simply awesome! Thorough, clear, theologically and biblically correct. The best ever!"
> *Col. E. H. (Jim) Ammerman, USA, Ret.*
> *President/Founder*
> *Chaplaincy of Full Gospel Churches*

"The fingerprints of the Holy Spirit are all over Dr. Stan Linzey's book. God will work through those who reach out to Him."
> *Dian Scott*
> *Former Assistant to Kathryn Khulman*

"Dr. Linzey has put into words the need and blessings of Pentecost. The Pentecostal movement needs this book."
Dr. Lemuel M. Boyles
> *Military Chaplain Endorser*
> *Pentecostal Church of God*

"This book will lift the believer into a life of power and joy."
> *Dr. O. Ray Williams, President and CEO*
> *International Correspondence and Radio Evangelism*

"Unusual, bold and thought provoking. Dr. Linzey answers questions you were afraid to ask."
> *Lana Heightley, Founder/Director*
> *Women With A Mission*

"If you read only one book on the Holy Spirit this year, let it be this one."
> *Dr. Frank S. Klapach, D.Min.*
> *Northwest College*

Comments

"This book is incredibly important in the ongoing discussion concerning the significance and rise of the Pentecostal Movement."

Rick C. Howard, Pastor
Peninsula Christian Center
Redwood City, California

Contents

Preface xix
Foreword xxi
Introduction xxv

PART I:
THE HOLY SPIRIT BAPTISM:
DOCTRINAL STATEMENT, DEFINITIONS AND
EXAMPLES..31

Chapter One: Nuclear Power at Sandia Base
    Definition of the Baptism with the Holy Spirit...........33
Chapter Two: Why Do They Wait?
    The Futility of Tarrying 53
Chapter Three: Cornelius and the Electronics Engineer
    Does everyone speak with tongues?............................63
Chapter Four: Fire in the Pentagon
    The Purpose of the Baptism in the Holy Spirit 81
Chapter Five: Is Someone's Life at Stake?
    Reasons to Speak in Tongues 97
Chapter Six: The Pebble in the Pond
    When Can the Believer Receive? 111
Chapter Seven: Can God Make a Mistake?
    Who May Receive? 125
Chapter Eight: Spiritual Secrets to God
    How to Manifest the Spirit? 133

Chapter Nine: The Altar Call
Is the News Good? 147
Epilogue: Is all this Necessary? 155

PART II:
QUESTIONS AND ANSWERS 157

Index to Questions

Question One: The Catholics and the Neo-Pentecostals have experienced the manifestations of the Sprit for only a short time and they appear much happier about it than we Pentecostals who have enjoyed this experience for a long time. May it be that we have had the blessing for too long, have had it too easy, and/or do not appreciate it as we should? 160

Question Two: Why do most prayer languages sound repetitious and why do some people's prayer languages sound alike? Should they not be more varied? Are we repeating ourselves over and over? 160

Question Three: If it is true that when a person speaks in tongues, it is his/her own spirit that speaks, and not the Holy Spirit speaking through him, (as we have so often heard), then how does my spirit know what to pray for? 161

Question Four: Can a person receive the baptism with the Holy Spirit without speaking in tongues? Please explain? 162

Question Five: May a person receive the gift of devotional tongues when he has no intention of discontinuing the use of tobacco or other drugs? 163

Question Six: Those who criticize the 'tongues-talkers' say that tongues are not needed today. They quote I Corinthians 13:8-10 as a proof text for their argument:

"That which is perfect" is the canon of Scripture, and since all truth is contained therein, tongues shall cease. How do you answer them? 164

Question Seven: Please explain what you mean when you say, "Practice your prayer language." 165

Question Eight: Is there such a thing as a counterfeit tongue? I have an acquaintance of the Mormon faith, which does not believe that Jesus, or the Holy Spirit, is God. However, she says that she speaks in tongues. How could these tongues be of God?..............................165

Question Nine: Please explain I Corinthians 14:13, "...the man who speaks in a tongue should pray that he may interpret what he says." 166

Question Ten: In reference to I Corinthians 14:23, when our church worships, we all pray in unknown tongues out loud, all together. How do we know that we are not doing what the Scripture says not to do? The first time I went to a church that did this, it scared me and turned me away as this Scripture said that it would. 167

Question Eleven: If a person should accept the Lord over a television program by phone, but does not follow up by going to church and being baptized, will he still go to heaven?..168

Question Twelve: Don't the Scriptures show that speaking with tongues must come from the Holy Spirit and not learned from 'practice?' 170

Question Thirteen: How does one receive the ability to give a message in tongues after having received his prayer language? Or, how do you know you are to give a message in tongues? 171

Question Fourteen: I Corinthians 14:15 states: "I will pray with my spirit, but I will also pray with my mind." Please explain. 173

Question Fifteen: If we each have a gift, and if everyone of us should exercise it once we realize what it is, could it be that some of us hinder the exercise of someone else's gift by either standing in the way or by doing too much in the church? How should leadership handle the placing of persons who feel that they know what their gifts are? 173

Question Sixteen: What did Jesus mean in John 20:22 when "He breathed on them, and said, 'Receive the Holy Spirit'? 174

Question Seventeen: Please explain Romans 8:26 and 27: In the same way, the Spirit helps us in our weakness. We do not know what we ought to pray, but the Spirit himself intercedes for us with groans that words cannot express. And he who searches our hearts knows the mind of the Spirit, because the Spirit intercedes for the saints in accordance with God's will 176

Question Eighteen: If a person has been filled with the Holy Spirit for years and is still hanging on to his old habits of the world such as drinking, abusing drugs, smoking, etc., or he believes that it is alright to do these things, should that person be placed in a position of leadership? If people are told that they can continue these habits and still make it to heaven, why give them [the habits] up? 176

Question Nineteen: When we pray in tongues, can Satan understand our prayer? 178

Question Twenty: People who speak against tongues argue that it should not be done because Jesus never spoke in tongues. How do you answer that? 179

Question Twenty-One: Is there any language that is unknown?' 179

Question Twenty-Two: In I Corinthians 13:1, Paul said, "If I speak in the tongues of men and of angels, but have not love, I am only a resounding gong or a clanging cymbal." What do you make of this? 180

Question Twenty-Three: Must one be baptized in water

before one may be baptized or filled with the Holy Spirit? 180

Question Twenty-Four: Why do you tell those who are seeking to manifest the Holy Spirit to repeat words from your own prayer language? Was this to help them break through their resistance to speaking in tongues? If only repetition of your words was spoken, is this a valid initial evidence of tongues for those instructed? 181

Question Twenty-Five: Why should I desire to speak with tongues? 183

Question Twenty-Six: Why do the Pentecostal churches put so much emphasis on tongues when it is the 'least' of the gifts? I praise God that I speak with tongues; however, there is so much more. We appear to get hung up on tongues. We should seek the power, not the tongues. 184

Question Twenty-Seven: I have received the baptism with the Holy Spirit and spoke in tongues at the time. I have not been able to pray in tongues since. Why is this? 185

Question Twenty-Eight: It is said that the Holy Spirit works in a gentlemanly fashion. Would He give a word of knowledge to someone whose heart it would disturb or trouble? 186

Question Twenty-Nine: Why is it that some people have a jubilant and strong experience when they manifest the Holy Spirit, while others struggle with it and even sometimes doubt whether or not they have ever received it? 187

Question Thirty: Please explain Acts 4:31 in light of Acts 2:4. After they prayed, the place where they were meeting was shaken. And they were all filled with the Holy Spirit and spoke the word of God boldly (Acts 4:31). All of them were filled with the Holy Spirit and began to speak in other tongues as the Spirit enabled them (Acts

2:4) 188
Question Thirty-One: If the baptism with the Holy Spirit [tongues manifestation] comes from within the believer, then what do the following expressions mean? ...tarry...until ye be endued with power from on high (Luke 24:49 KJV). I will pour out my Spirit upon all flesh" (cf. Joel 2:28 with Acts 2:17 KJV). The Holy Ghost fell on all of them...On the Gentiles also was poured out the gift of the Holy Ghost (Acts 10:44 and 45 KJV). The Holy Ghost came on them..." (Acts 19:6 KJV). 189
Question Thirty-Two: Please explain the gift of prophecy, diverse kinds of tongues, and interpretation of tongues. How do we receive these gifts? 191
Question Thirty-Three: Please explain how I, a Spirit-filled, baptized believer, went through deliverance of evil spirits, and how my wife also went through the same. ...193
Question Thirty-Four: Is speaking in tongues a gift or a manifestation of the Spirit? If it is a gift, I understand that God will not take it away from a person. If it is a manifestation, the how can the Holy Spirit be manifested in someone who is a backslider? 195
Question Thirty-Five: I believe the Holy Spirit is received at salvation. Then what is the baptism with the Holy Spirit? In simple language, what is it? 197
Question Thirty-Six: Can children receive the baptism with the Holy Spirit? Can they speak in tongues? 197
Question Thirty-Seven: How can we receive the power to heal someone through the laying on of hands? 198
Question Thirty-Eight: Please explain the gift of the Word of Knowledge and how it is received. 199
Question Thirty-Nine: Is it scriptural to lay on hands for the reception of the Spirit? 200
Question Forty: It seems that every time you pray with someone, he easily manifests the Holy Spirit by speaking

Contents

with tongues. Is this true in all your meetings? Have there been occasions in which some did not receive? If not, why not? How do you help them? 201

Question Forty-One: Many Christians in leadership positions in the non-Pentecostal churches show evidence in their daily lives that they are filled with the Spirit, but they do not speak with tongues. We know people who practice tongues on a regular basis whose lives do not demonstrate that they are filled with the Spirit. Why is this? 201

Question Forty-Two: Is there an artificial or counterfeit tongues experience? Are there some tongues that tongues-speakers experience that are not the real thing? 202

Question Forty-Three: Where in the world did some churches come up with the doctrine that tongues are of the devil? 204

Question Forty-Four: Why do some people use I Corinthians 13:8 to excuse themselves from the baptism with the Holy Spirit? 206

Question Forty-Five: Can we pray in tongues as a means of spiritual warfare? 206

Question Forty-Six: Will a person who gives messages in tongues also eventually be able to interpret his own messages? 207

Question Forty-Seven: Is it possible to discern whether a person who is speaking in tongues is in the flesh or in the Spirit? 207

Question Forty-Eight: Is it scriptural to have prayer for a refilling of the Holy Spirit? Sometimes I get so dry. 208

Question Forty-Nine: Is 'dancing in the spirit' scriptural? If it is scriptural, what is it? 209

Question Fifty: What does it mean to be 'slain in the Spirit?' 210

Question Fifty-One: After receiving the manifestation of the Spirit, is it scriptural for a person to receive a special filling to empower him for a specific ministry? 211

Question Fifty-Two: I have been filled with the Spirit a short time, and sometimes when I pray, I wonder if I am really speaking in tongues, or making up the words myself. Am I speaking a language, or just a bunch of sounds I put together? How do I now if it is really my prayer language? Also, could this be the devil trying to discourage me? 212

Question Fifty-Three: Paul said in I Corinthians 12:31 that we are to seek the greater gifts. What are they? 213

References 215
Index..221

Preface

There are always many people who stand behind a work such as this and it would be impossible to mention all the names of those who taught me what I know about the inner workings of the Holy Spirit. The numerous persons who came forward for prayer to receive the Blessing of the Spirit will never know of the opportunities they provided for me to study how the blessed Spirit fills His people. However, I wish to mention those that I am obviously more aware of, those who counseled, discussed with me, and provided numerous points of insight. In this regard, I appreciate reverend David A. Womack, Director of Acts in Action, and former pastor of Twin Palms Assembly of God in San Jose, California, for continually urging me to put my thoughts and passion into print for the Church. His insights and suggestions have been of great value.

My daughters, the late Virginia Darnelle Lemons and Professor Sharon F. Linzey, have spent many hours reading and correcting the manuscript and have made valuable literary suggestions that have given form to the work. My sons, Reverends James F. Linzey and Paul E. Linzey, have urged me to complete the volume, stressing the need of the church for this study. I thank them. To the many officials, pastors and churches in the Assemblies of God with whom I have ministered and for whom I have great respect and admiration, I express my heartfelt thanks for the experiences we have shared.

The Full Gospel Business Men's Fellowship, International has given me an open door to their chapters and national conventions across the nation for ministry, and we share in their experiences and successes. Mr. Ronnie Svenhard, International President of the Business Men's Fellowship, has been most kind in extending to me an open invitation to minister in Oakland. This venue has expanded the scope of this ministry and I thank him. The Reverend James C. Davis, Jr., Director of David Ministries in Oakland, has provided counsel and encouragement to me to finish the work. I am grateful to him.

To Verna May, my faithful wife and companion of sixty years, I express my greatest appreciation for her prayers, suggestions, and patience as I have endeavored to work and rework this writing.

For all of their help I am grateful and with all of their help this study has been able to come to fruition. I, of course, take full responsibility for any errors or oversights in this work.

Stanford E. Linzey, Jr.
Escondido, California
August 2002

Foreword

There are three essentials for good writing: a disciplined talent, something meaningful to say, and the determined motivation to create form out of chaos and publish it in print. Dr. Stanford E. Linzey possesses all three of these vital qualifications and has written a significant book that will define for Pentecostal and Charismatic Christians the meaning of spiritual experience. He will also clarify the relationship between the person and work of the Holy Spirit. Not since Donald Gee has any Pentecostal writer analyzed and explained the operation of the Holy Spirit as does Dr. Linzey in this new book.

That he is a talented and intellectually serious writer may be seen in his many magazine articles and his widely read book, Pentecost in the Pentagon. His pamphlet, "Why I Believe in the Baptism of the Holy Spirit," has been distributed widely and translated into other languages. He received his doctorate from Fuller Theological Seminary in Pasadena after studying at several seminaries including the Harvard Divinity School.

Stanford Linzey is an American hero who was aboard the USS YORKTOWN when it was torpedoed and sunk by the Japanese in the Battle of Midway in World War Two. He went on to become a chaplain in the U.S. Navy and rose to the rank of captain. This made him one of the highest-ranking military officers in the Assemblies of God. When he was Command Chaplain in the USS CORAL SEA, so many sailors were saved and filled with the Holy Spirit that it was called, 'The Pentecostal ship.'

Since retiring from the Navy in 1974, Stan and his wife, Verna, have traveled extensively in the United States and abroad holding Holy Spirit Seminars in churches and colleges. Many thousands of people have received the Baptism with the Holy Spirit under his ministry. As pastor of the Twin Palms Assembly of God in San Jose, I would invite Stan to teach his four-day seminar every 12 to 18 months, and each time he did we had 25 to 35 people speak in other tongues for the first time. People respond to his sensible presentation without the long struggles that many have mistakenly associated with the Baptism with the Holy Spirit in times past.

Yet, with all his public preaching, Dr. Linzey had never put into writing his great life work on the ministry and operation of the Holy Spirit. Every time he came to my church I would ask how his book was progressing. I pushed, prodded and cajoled him. I told him that any old seaman worth his salt would buy a computer and get his ideas down for the rest of the world to see. And now he has written a most valuable contribution to our literature on the Holy Spirit.

Because of the depth of his background as a chaplain and an evangelist, and the breadth of his theological education and experience with many denominational and interchurch groups and organizations, Dr. Linzey is able to communicate across religious lines that would present barriers to many other speakers and writers. He addresses with equal ease such diverse audiences as military personnel, businessmen, Fundamentalist and Evangelical pastors, and even strangers who happen into conversation with him. The outcome is nearly always the same—they soon speak with other tongues.

Foreword

Of course not everyone will agree with this book. After all, why should anyone write a book (or for that matter read it) if the author and the reader agree? The fact is that Dr. Linzey has helped many people to understand the Baptism with the Holy Spirit and to receive this wonderful gift of God, manifesting their experience of speaking with other tongues. I believe that time will show that what was once one man's comprehension of biblical truth will become the generally accepted belief of us all.

David A. Womack
Green Valley, Arizona
August 2002

Introduction

This book addresses many practical matters related to the Holy Spirit, His manifestations in the Church body, and His manifestations in the lives of individual believers today. It deals particularly with the vocal gifts given in I Corinthians 12. At first glance one might be tempted to think that I have overstated the case for speaking with tongues. However, serious students of the Holy Spirit will hopefully understand my goal to bring this manifestation into sharper focus for the Church and Christian believers. The experiential aspect is unapologetically emphasized for the simple reason that people need to experience the fullness of the Holy Spirit. Christian believers need all the help they can get to empower them to live vital and powerful lives as witnesses to the blessed Hope of the world.

According to David Barrett, editor of the World Christian Encyclopedia (1982), there were 27 million Pentecostal and Charismatic adherents worldwide in 1982. The International Bulletin of Missionary Research reported in June 1991 that there were 382 million Pentecostal and Charismatic members in the world. This group was reported to increase at the rate of 19 million members annually. At the present time this number has grown to over 524 million. There are over

29 million Charismatics in China. One of every four Christians worldwide is a charismatic, and two of every three Pentecostal believers live in third world countries!

George Gallup has reported that about 15 percent of the Episcopal clergy consider themselves to be Charismatic. Among the Roman Catholics, 1,500 priests and 25 bishops identify as Charismatic, as do about 7 million Catholic laymen and women. There are over 80 million Pentecostal Catholics worldwide.

About 10 percent of the ministers of the Missouri Lutheran Synod are estimated to be Charismatic, and the revival in Latin America is 90 percent Pentecostal in constituency. A generation ago Henry Pitt Van Dusen, President of Union Theological Seminary, predicted that the last half of the Twentieth Century would be remembered in Church history as the "age of Pentecostal-Charismatic Christianity."

It is interesting to note that some Charismatic groups do not think it necessary to speak with tongues when one manifests the baptism with the Holy Spirit. Likewise, it should be noted that the *experience* of speaking in tongues is often disconnected to the notion of being 'filled with the Spirit.' I would like to urge all of our Christian brothers and sisters who feel this way to consider the many benefits of manifesting the Spirit through speaking in tongues. The benefits are many and you may be in for a big surprise.

We Pentecostals, who do believe that speaking in tongues is the manifestation of the Holy Spirit, have our own problems. In Pentecostal churches in America today, it has been estimated that perhaps as many as fifty percent of our people have not manifested the baptism with the Holy Spirit, speaking with tongues. Moreover, many appear to be apathetic toward the work of the Spirit and His gifts. The Reverend Thomas E. Trask, General Superintendent of the Assemblies of God, said recently that his church might be more Pentecostal in doctrine than it is in practice. This is a telling relation about what may be happening within the largest Pentecostal denomination in history today.

Some have said that within one decade there will no longer be any preaching on the baptism with the Holy Spirit in our churches. This should be disturbing for Pentecostals who have a century-old tradition of manifesting the Holy Spirit with the evidence of speaking in tongues.

Let me be clear. We believe that the baptism with the Holy Spirit is the same today in manifestation and demonstration as it was for the early Church in the Book of Acts and that it is intended for the believer now as it was intended for the believers in the early Church.

The questions that form the chapters in Part I were derived from an interview with the religion editor of the *San Diego Union-Tribune*. His persistence and skillful interviewing enabled me to clarify my thesis and bring it into focus. As a result, he published five columns on the subject and I was on my way to clarifying the relationship of speaking in tongues (manifesting the Spirit) with the theology of the Holy Spirit as it is perceived, or in my opinion should be perceived, by informed Pentecostals.

For thirty years I have conducted seminars in churches, colleges and Bible studies nationwide and around the world. I believe that the method that I explicate in these chapters is the correct course of action for those intent on exploring the Spirit-filled life, or what we Pentecostals call the 'Walk in the Spirit.' Even for those with differing opinions to the classical Pentecostal position, speaking in tongues has many benefits that those who love the Lord should not denigrate. Our motivation should be to experience all that God has in store for us. It is in this light that the following pages should be considered. Unless otherwise noted, all Scripture references are taken from the New International Version.

In my ministry alone nearly 20,000 men, women, boys and girls have manifested the Holy Spirit—speaking with tongues—as the Spirit gave them utterance, that is, after prayer and the laying on of hands.

I unapologetically emphasize the experience of speaking with tongues in this study. While Orthodox Christians may believe in the doctrine of the Holy Spirit academically, there are those who deny the supernatural phenomena associated with it in terms of its gifts and outworking. In this study my aim is to be true to New Testament Christianity in all its hope and power, while at the same time doing justice to Pentecostal theology, early Church history and the believing Christian who needs all the help he or she can get to be a powerful witness and effective Christian in the third millennium. Elton Trueblood once said that there was no such thing as a non-witnessing Christian. He considered that to be a contradiction in terms. If he is right, and I believe he is, then we believers must do some introspection individually and collectively to find out where and why we are lacking in power in our lives—power to impact others for Christ, and power to live holy and righteous lives in their own right. Instead of skepticism and cynicism, let us be open to all of what God has available to us. Let us be filled with the Spirit.

Part I is devoted to answering basic questions about the Holy Spirit and His manifestations. Each chapter opens with a true-life experience followed by a discussion of relevant theological implications and explanations from the Scriptures.

Part II is devoted to questions and answers that have been asked during our seminars around the world concerning the Holy Spirit and His manifestation gifts. This section should prove helpful to pastors, teachers, churches, Sunday school classes and Bible study groups as they seek to understand what role that the experience of speaking in tongues has in the life of the Christian today. It can be used as a ready reference for those who want to know what the Bible has to say on this important subject.

May these pages contribute to that end.

Stanford E. Linzey, Jr.
Escondido, California
August 2002

PART ONE

*BAPTISM:
DOCTRINAL STATEMENT, DEFINITIONS
AND EXAMPLES*

Chapter One

NUCLEAR POWER AT SANDIA BASE

Definition of the Baptism with the Holy Spirit

I received orders to attend a nuclear seminar for military chaplains at Sandia Base in Albuquerque, New Mexico. The Department of Defense conducted these seminars annually to brief senior chaplains from the Armed Forces on the capabilities of our nuclear arsenal. On each occasion the Chief of Chaplains from one of the branches of the Armed Forces addressed the group. I boarded a Navy DC-3 and flew to Albuquerque.

Commander R. L. Warren, a Presbyterian chaplain, met me on the tarmac. We had entered the Navy together fifteen years earlier and had become good friends over the years. He had come from Washington, D.C. to represent the Navy Chief of Chaplains at this nuclear seminar. After brief greetings we went up to his room in the bachelor officers quarters to reminisce and catch up with each other.

After chatting for a few moments, Bob said, "Stan, I've been 'tapped.'"

"Tapped? What do you mean, 'tapped'?" I prodded.

"I received the baptism in the Holy Spirit," he said.

"Did you speak with tongues?" I probed.

"No, but I received it!" Bob insisted.

"Bob, when you receive the baptism with the Holy Spirit, you should speak with tongues like they did in the Book of Acts," I told him.

"Is that right?"

"Yes, it is," I responded. I did not feel like pressing this point further at the moment, so after visiting some more, I retired to my room.

However, the Lord began to impress upon me that I should lead Bob into the 'experience' of the Holy Spirit. Bob had always been a man of prayer, and if God were to bless him with the infilling of the Spirit, he would be prepared for greater service in the years ahead.

The next morning we met for breakfast. Seminar lectures followed and we were tied up in sessions all day. That evening we went to Old Town for a spicy Mexican dinner and then returned to his room to resume our discussion about the Holy Spirit.

After some time I said, "Bob, when you receive the baptism with the Holy Spirit, you should speak with tongues like the disciples did on the Day of Pentecost." And then I blatantly said, "If you wish, I can lay hands on you and pray, and in a few moments Jesus will baptize you with the Spirit, and you will speak with tongues."

"Do you mean that?" He asked.

"I do indeed." We were standing as we spoke, and after a few moments, he put his hands on his hips as if to challenge me. Then, as if giving a military order, he said, "All right! Do it!"

"All right, kneel down!" I responded with an equivalent military-style directive. We both knelt at one of the bunks and began to pray side-by-side. I put my arm on his shoulder and prayed: "God, please baptize Bob with the Holy Spirit!"

After a few moments Bob raised his hands and the Spirit came upon him. He began to speak with tongues at the top of his voice. It was 11:30 p.m., and all was supposed to be quiet in the quarters at this late hour. But we were having our own nuclear seminar, a hilarious prayer and praise meeting, and I was exuberantly praising God along with Bob.

All of a sudden, we both stopped praying and faced each other and began to laugh—a truly holy laughter! Then he sobered up and asked, "Can I speak in tongues again?" I assured him that he could, and he did so for another few moments. After more praise and worship I went to my room.

We met the next morning for breakfast, and as he approached me, he yelled across the lawn, "Stan, I went to bed speaking with tongues, and I woke up speaking with tongues. I can speak with tongues any time I wish!"

"That's right, Bob," I said. "You surely can."

Chaplain Warren served in the Navy for over 30 years leading men and women to Christ, and after this experience at Sandia Base, he also led others into the fullness of the Holy Spirit. He later wrote of the effect of the baptism with the Holy Spirit on his ministry:

It has greatly enhanced my ministry of preaching salvation. While serving as chaplain in the USS COLUMBUS, 150 men came to Christ and many received the baptism with the Holy Spirit. While serving as chaplain at the U.S. Naval Shipyard, Mare Island, California, over 400 service people came to Christ.

Bob attained the rank of Captain in the Navy and after he retired Pat Robertson chose him to serve on the staff of the 700 Club in Virginia Beach where he served as a vice-president and International Director of 'Operation Blessing.' He held this post for several years and because of his spiritual experience and position of influence, has been used of God to meet with many heads of state. Operation Blessing has assisted millions of people around the world with food and clothing. Jesus had baptized this Presbyterian Chaplain with the Holy Spirit and prepared him for this great ministry.

What is the Baptism with the Holy Spirit?

The concept of the baptism with the Holy Spirit is a complex one. Consequently it is confusing to many people. Often times those who speak with tongues do not even understand its operation. How is this strange phenomenon to be understood? Let us start at the beginning and break down what we know of this complex gift so that we may grasp it more easily.

The baptism with the Holy Spirit is the reception of the Spirit, which manifests itself in speaking with tongues. Speaking in tongues is the outward manifestation of the inward experience of the Spirit. This is a New Testament phenomenon and every Christian denomination in America today has its own Charismatic wing. Rather than have new 'Reformations' and denominational splits, the Roman Catholic Church and the mainline Protestant denominations have had to make room for this fresh move of the Spirit in modern times—often called 'NeoPentecostalism' or the 'Charismatic Renewal'—to keep from losing members to Pentecostal groups or denominations which allow for this type of freedom of the Spirit. The Roman Catholic Church has embraced this wing ever since it broke out at the University of Notre Dame in the Sixties. The Pope put Cardinal Suenens from Belgium in charge of the movement, lest the new Charismatics leave the Church.

We see in the Book of Acts that when people accepted Christ as their Savior, it was the common practice for them to speak with tongues. This was the normal Christian experience once the Holy Spirit was given at Pentecost. We will observe closely how this happened as we go along.

The reception of the Spirit, with its accompanying

manifestation, was an objective practice and observance in the early Church. The Church expected one to manifest the Spirit and the new believer readily did so at the time of his conversion. Contextually, we can surmise that speaking with tongues was the observable, uniform evidence of the baptism with the Holy Spirit in the early church. This manifestation was the initial evidence of one's having received the Spirit, and it took place at conversion.

The first mention of Spirit Baptism in the Bible was made by John the Baptist in Matthew 3:11. He said,

I baptize you with water for repentance. But after me will come one who is more powerful than I, whose sandals I am not fit to carry. He will baptize you with the Holy Spirit and with fire.

Israel had always practiced water baptisms, which were ceremonial cleansings or purification rites. The concept of a *baptism* with the *Spirit*, however, was new to New Testament converts. This is the first use of the term 'baptism with the Holy Spirit.'[1]

The prophet foretold of the time when God would bestow His Spirit on His people. Joel said,

And afterward, I will pour out my spirit upon all people. Your sons and your daughters will prophesy, your old men will dream dreams, your young men will see visions. Even on my servants, both men and women, I will pour out of my spirit in those days (Joel 2:28, 29).

Joel prophesied of the messianic period when Messiah would come and pour out His Spirit on all flesh. In the Old Testament era generally only those in positions of leadership in Israel experienced the *moving* of the Spirit. For example, kings, priests, judges, prophets and the various deliverers or redeemers who came along from time to time often received a special "enduement from on high."[2] The common people were only followers in the camp. They did as they were told by their leaders and were expected to obey.

All of this changed when Messiah came. Now the Holy Spirit would lead them all.

Jeremiah spoke of a New Covenant when God would put His Law in the hearts of His people (Jeremiah 31:31-33). He said,
> The time is coming, declares the Lord, when I will make a new covenant with the house of Israel and with the house of Judah. It will not be like the covenant I made with their forefathers when I took them by the hand to lead them out of Egypt, because they broke my covenant, though I was a husband to them, declares the Lord. This is the covenant I will make with the house of Israel after that time, declares the Lord. I will put my law in their minds and write it on their hearts. I will be their God, and they will be my people.

The prophet foretold of the Messianic age when Jesus the Messiah would come to earth. This time was not to be until 40 days after Jesus ascended into heaven, a new era that theologians and historians call the New Testament Church age.

But let us return to the Old Testament age for some historical background and social context. In the Old Testament period under the Law the people of God were not able to follow the will of God implicitly and completely due to the innate sinfulness of human nature and the imperfection of the flesh. The Commandments, blessed as they were, did not, nor could they, provide the inner power and strength necessary to conform to the mandates of a holy God.[3] If anything, the Law aggravated man's sinful nature and tended to bring out the worst in him.[4] Parents understand that often when you tell a child not to touch some thing you can be sure that he will touch it—and the sooner the better! If he never thought of it before, he will certainly think of it now. You have put the thought in the child's mind. His natural tendency will be to disobey. This is a simplistic example to demonstrate the 'fallen' nature of mankind. Paul wrestled with his dilemma and expressed it forcibly when he said,

> I found that the very commandment that was intended to bring life actually brought death. For sin, seizing the opportunity afforded by the commandment, deceived me, and through the commandment put me to death" (Romans 7:10, 11).

The writer to the Hebrews said, "For the law made nothing perfect, and a better hope is introduced, by which we draw near to God" (7:19).

Since God's people are called to live righteously and in holiness, and since our depraved nature makes it impossible to do this in our own strength, God in his mercy gives us the very thing we need to serve Him. It necessitates the indwelling Holy Spirit to bring about righteous and holy living in our beings. Only He can do it. He gives us the very thing He asks of us.

According to John's prophecy, Jesus Christ is the One who baptizes with the Spirit (Matthew 3:11). John said,

> I baptize you with water for repentance. But after me will come one who is more powerful than I, whose sandals I am not fit to carry. He will baptize you with the Holy Spirit and with fire.

Another reading states, "He will baptize you with the fiery Holy Spirit." Here we see from John's own words the proof that God gives His Spirit to man to allow mankind to serve Him and meet His expectations.

Incidentally, this is the first mention of Spirit baptism in the Bible. The Jews had always known of the Holy Spirit from the time of Moses and the prophets, but never before had there been the concept of a 'baptism with the Holy Spirit.' John brings this into focus for us in the passage cited. This baptism with the Spirit is equated with the reception of the Spirit. Its initial physical manifestation is speaking with tongues, as we shall see below. The paradigm is established from the beginning on the Day of Pentecost.

At this juncture we take note that there are two baptisms, (1) baptism in water and (2) baptism in the Spirit. Men baptize in and with the element of water, while Jesus baptizes men and women with and in the 'element' of the Spirit. However, we should also recognize that there is a third baptism, and that is the baptism into the body of Christ.

For we were all baptized by one Spirit into one body—whether Jews or Greeks, slave or free—and we were all given the one Spirit to drink (1 Corinthians 12:13).

The Holy Spirit is the Person of God on earth Who deals with men and women and brings them to the knowledge of Jesus. He leads them into repentance and acceptance of Jesus for forgiveness of their sins. This is what we commonly refer to as salvation. When people make a profession of faith in Jesus, the Holy Spirit puts, places, sets, or baptizes them into the body of Christ. The term *baptize* is used here in a metaphorical sense, meaning to 'set-in', or to 'place-in.' The Holy Spirit is the Agent in this baptism and the 'element' is the body of Christ.

Accordingly, we must understand that all who have accepted Jesus Christ as Lord and Savior—regardless of church affiliation—have been baptized into the body of Christ. This cannot be overemphasized. We are all family, belonging to the same body, and belonging to one Head, Jesus Christ. In this sense, all have had the Spirit of Christ since conversion. To miss this point is equivalent to calling co-believers 'pagans.'

When Paul said, "we were all given the one Spirit to drink" (1 Corinthians 12:13), he is suggesting that when we came to Jesus, we took a drink, or a sip, of the Holy Spirit.

Paul said in Romans 8:9, "If anyone does not have the

Spirit of Christ, he does not belong to Christ." Paul also said,
> Do you not know that your body is a temple of the Holy Spirit, who is in you, whom you have received from God? You are not your own (1 Corinthians 6:19).

We must recognize that all believers receive, or partake of, the Spirit when they come to Jesus Christ. I believe that the pattern of evidence is laid down before us in Scripture to support the firm belief and expectation that believers could at the time of salvation manifest the Spirit's presence by speaking with tongues—*if they knew that they could!* Unfortunately, many have been told that speaking in tongues is not for believers today and that they should not expect it. Many fine preachers, ministries, and Christian organizations teach this misconception to believers in their sermons, books, and even on the web, and hence unaware or innocent believers remain ignorant of this awesome and wonderful experience.

Note that in the book of Acts believers spoke in tongues upon receiving the Spirit. This normally happened in one of two ways. Sometimes it was the result of a sovereign act of God (see Acts 2, 10). That is, no human agency or ministrations were involved. God simply moved on His own initiative and poured out His Spirit at Pentecost and at the home of Cornelius the Roman Centurion to whom Peter preached. God in a sovereign manner simply poured out His Spirit.

The second way believers came to speak in tongues was through the laying on of hands. In Acts 19 we note the ministry of the laying on of hands for the impartation of the Sprit. Paul led the Ephesian Baptists to Jesus Christ, and then laid hands on them for imparting the Spirit. The result was that they spoke with tongues. Here, human agency (Paul) was involved. Both methods are appropriate today.

There are two equally good terms that refer to the event surrounding speaking in one's heavenly language. They are:

'receive the baptism with the Holy Spirit' and, 'manifest the Holy Spirit.' I prefer to use the latter term because, as already pointed out, believers have the Spirit of Christ and have had the Spirit since their conversion. Both are good biblical terms.

To say to a person, "receive the baptism with the Holy Spirit," indicates to some believers that they are going to receive the Spirit, which they think they do not currently have. This is not accurate, for as we have already pointed out, all Christians have received the Spirit (Romans 8:9; I Corinthians 6:19).

One receives the Spirit once and for all when he accepts Jesus. Jesus said, "[He is] to abide with you forever" (John 14:16). So, there is no second *reception* of the Spirit indicated in the Bible. They are not going to receive the Spirit a *second* time. They will simply manifest His indwelling presence.

To help the man in the pew desire the experience with the Holy Spirit, I have found it is better to encourage him by using the term 'manifest the Holy Spirit.' One can at the time of laying on of hands with prayer (or, in his private prayer 'closet'), manifest the Spirit by speaking in tongues. This removes the needless, fearful and uneasy feelings some people may have of receiving an additional supernatural experience after conversion.

Early Pentecostals sometimes believed in two 'stages' of spiritual development: (1) conversion and (2) sanctification. I think today we understand that the whole of life is one of purification, refining and being conformed to Christ's image (see Romans 8:29 and II Peter 3:18). Jesus said,

> If you, then, though you are evil, know how to give good gifts to your children, how much more will your father in heaven give the Holy Spirit to those who ask him? (Luke 11:13).

The account of the outpouring of the Spirit at that first New Testament Pentecost (40 days after the ascension) is given in Acts 2:1-4. It reads:

> And when the day of Pentecost came, [the Feast of Pentecost in Jewish tradition] they were all together in one place. Suddenly a sound like the blowing of a violent wind came from heaven and filled the whole house where they were sitting. They saw what seemed to be tongues of fire that separated and came to rest on each of them. All of them were filled with the Holy Spirit and began to speak in other tongues as the Spirit enabled them.

Now this is quite a story. We can see how outrageous the behavior of the early believers must have been by the fact that they were accused of being drunk. We will come back to this later.

John had said, "I baptize you with water for repentance...he will baptize you with the Holy Spirit and with fire" (Matthew 3:11). Jesus followed up on this when He said, "For John baptized with water, but in a few days you will be baptized with the Holy Spirit" (Acts 1:5).

So we may deduce that the outpouring of the Spirit at Pentecost is called, in name and terminology, the 'baptism with the Holy Spirit.' And note: this shall be the term used, and the experience followed, by the Church and Her believers for the ensuing two-thousand plus years of existence, or until Jesus comes again. The paradigm is laid out clearly and we will see this pattern repeated.

Jesus received the promised Holy Spirit from the Father when He was exalted at God's right hand, and poured out the Spirit upon His people on this first Pentecost after the resurrection. Thus, He fulfilled His promise to send the Holy Spirit as Counselor and Teacher (see John 14:16 and 15:26). Peter said,

> God has raised this Jesus to life, and we are all witnesses of the fact. Exalted to the right hand of God, he has received from the Father the promised Holy Spirit and has poured out what you now see and hear (Acts 2:32, 33).

After His death and resurrection, Jesus was received into heaven and was exalted at God's right hand. F. F. Bruce wrote,

> He, who had earlier received the Spirit for the public discharge of his own messianic ministry, had now received the same Spirit to impart to His representatives on earth, in order that they might continue the ministry that he began.[5]

Bruce adds, "The impartation of the Spirit with the attendance of sensible signs was a further vindication of the claim that He was the exalted Messiah."[6]

The Holy Spirit was given to the world of believers on the occasion of that first Pentecost after Christ's resurrection, and He has been in the world since that time, filling and indwelling believers. God has always been in His world. He created it and has never given up on it, even though man has fallen, and continues to fail miserably. But now He has entered into the hearts of His people in a new and living way, revealing personal contact with them through and by means of the Holy Spirit.[7]

Let's look at the ancient Hebrew feasts for a moment and see how Pentecost fits into Old Testament theology. During the Old Testament era, Israel observed three feasts annually: Passover, Pentecost, and Tabernacles. The Passover commemorated the Jews' deliverance and exodus from Egypt under the hand of Moses. The Israelites were commanded to put the blood of lambs on their doorposts so that when the death angel came down to slay the first-born of man and animal in Egypt, the first-born of the Israelites would be spared. The Death Angel passed over each home marked by the blood, hence the term, Passover.[8] The Passover is a highly significant event to even the most secularized of Jews up to this day. Christ was crucified on the Passover, "The Lamb slain from the foundation of the world" (Revelation 13:8). Thus He fulfilled that feast day with the sacrifice of His own body, negating any future need to sacrifice animals. He was the eternal sacrifice.

Pentecost gets its name and meaning from the Greek word *pente*, which means 'fifty.' The Feast of Pentecost was celebrated fifty days after the feast of Passover. It was a harvest festival (see Deuteronomy 16). From ages past, the feast of Pentecost had commemorated the giving of the Law at Sinai 1,500 years before Christ. The Spirit descended on Pentecost, thus fulfilling that feast day and signifying the closing of the age of the Law. It ushered in the New Testament era of Messiah, or the dispensation of grace, sometimes referred to as the 'Church Age,' or the 'Dispensation of the Holy Spirit.' Christian theologians recognize this day as the birthday of the Church. It was a New Day indeed!

On the third feast—that of Tabernacles—the Jews normally observed in the seventh or eighth month of the Jewish calendar. This was the feast of Ingathering, generally held around the Temple—a celebration of thanksgiving for the harvest (Deuteronomy 16).

If at all possible, all males of mature age were to go to Jerusalem three times a year for these three principal feasts. This showed that though Israel was made up of many tribes, she was one nation united by a common heritage, practice and religion.

The Jewish nation had a glorious history. The God of the universe had called her to be His chosen Nation, first electing Abraham, then his descendants Isaac and Jacob, and continuing the lineage through the twelve sons of Jacob and their posterity: twelve tribes, yet one nation.

Moses, the Lawgiver and deliverer, had molded them into a cohesive national union and led them out of Egypt into the Land of Promise. They had much to be thankful for, though as we can see from their history, they often forgot the great and mighty things God did for them.

Of the three great feasts, two have been fulfilled to date. Christ was crucified on the feast of Passover, illustrating the infinite price paid for man's deliverance from sin. The Holy Spirit was poured out on Pentecost, thus fulfilling Joel's prophecy, "I will pour out my Spirit on all people" (Joel 2:28). Furthermore, the New Covenant that Jeremiah referred to in Chapter 31:33 was established: "...I will put my law in their minds, and write it on their hearts. I will be their God and they will be my people."

One great feast—that of Tabernacles, or 'Ingathering'—has yet to be fulfilled. I sometimes wonder if the fulfillment of this great event could possibly be waiting for the Ingathering of the Church, or the 'rapture,' when Jesus comes back for His own. We could very well celebrate this third feast with Messiah Himself!

The first Pentecost in Jerusalem after the resurrection was an awesome event. Perhaps one-and-a-half million Jews from all over the Roman Empire were there for this feast. This was going to be a special feast. Jesus had instructed them for forty days after the resurrection about the Kingdom of God. They were now to become active participants in Kingdom work. In order to do the work of the Kingdom, they would need added spiritual strength beyond their human capabilities. Jesus would provide the necessary power. Remember, He provides the ability to do what He commands. He said,

> I am going to send you what my Father has promised; but stay in the city until you have been clothed with power from on high (Luke 2:49).

He then added:
> You will receive power when the Holy Spirit comes upon you; and you will be my witnesses in Jerusalem, and in all Judea and Samaria, and to the ends of the earth (Acts 1:8).

The disciples waited ten days for Pentecost to come, waiting for the promised Holy Spirit. They likely wondered as to the nature of this spiritual power. What was it to be? How would it be imparted? And when? How would we recognize it when it comes? Would this be a new thing?

They did not yet understand that though Jesus had left them He was going to return to them in the person and power of the Holy Spirit to indwell them. His indwelling presence would provide them His power, the "all authority in heaven and in earth" (see Matthew 28:18). What Jesus could not do for the disciples as the external Christ, He would do for them and in them as the indwelling internal and eternal Christ.

Though they did not know what to expect, it happened nonetheless and they recognized it. How could they not? The Spirit came! Things would never be the same! There was a sound as of a stormy blast, a rushing mighty wind, and the appearance of a flash of fire. Fire, like wind, was symbolic of the divine Presence. Originally the tongues were as one mighty flame of fire. Then they parted and rested on each believer, a token of divine favor.

On that first post-resurrection Pentecost, as they were worshipping in their native tongues in the Temple (Luke 24:53), the Holy Spirit came upon them and "all of them were filled with the Holy Spirit and began to speak in other tongues as the spirit enabled them (Acts 2:4).

This is what they had been waiting for! This was new and different! Nothing like this had ever happened before. As the Word was made flesh in the person of Jesus, now the Holy Spirit was revealed in words of humans, through their speech. This was a New Testament phenomenon. With the Filling of the Holy Spirit, the disciples received the power Jesus had promised. The new Spirit of power is portrayed time and time again in the actions and conduct of the early New Testament Church throughout the book of Acts. While they once cowered in fear and denied the Christ, now they were bold and unafraid. Nothing but the Spirit of God could effect so great a transformation!

Boldness replaced timidity; fearlessness replaced fear; ability replaced inability; strength replaced weakness; believers were edified (see I Corinthians 14:4), and faith replaced unbelief. All by the power of the Holy Spirit.

This boldness is first seen in the Apostle Peter who had miserably denied the Christ during the latter's arrest. Now we see him defending the early Church against the charge of drunkenness. Where was the fear? Where was the doubt? It was to be no more. No more cowardice. As a result of his boldness in preaching on that first Pentecost, 3,000 people were converted to Christ and the Church was birthed. This is power. May God grant the Church that same Power today.

This phenomenon raised great consternation among the onlookers, however. Never had anything like this happened before during any feast. The believers were acting strangely, perhaps even in a giddy fashion. Moreover, they were speaking in tongues, languages they had not learned. How was it that these Galileans, the unschooled or unlearned Jews, were "declaring the wonders of God" (Acts 2:11) in various recognized and understood human languages of the known world? We need to understand that the tongues spoken at Pentecost were not gibberish or irrational babbling due to a frenetic mental state as some antagonists may claim. They were the many and various nationally known languages spoken in the Roman Empire at the time. The term *glossais* in the Greek text (Acts 2:4) clarifies this, as the word refers to human languages. The gathered crowd at Pentecost heard the disciples speak in human national languages that they had not learned. The crowd understood them for "We hear them declaring the wonders of God in our own tongues" (Acts 2:11).

Luke clarifies it further for us in Acts 2:6. The text reads, "each one heard them speaking in his own dialect." In this instance the Greek word *dialekto* is used. Thus, familiar human languages were spoken and understood by those gathering around the spectacle.

Paul Tournier, the eminent Swiss psychiatrist, noted the validity of the tongues experience for modern Christian believers today when he wrote:

> Glossalalia, or speaking with tongues, which played such an important part [in the early church], and which is still found in some modern communities, appears to answer to the need of the Spirit to express the inexpressible, to carry the dialogue with God beyond the narrow limits of clearly intelligible language.[9]

Not having a clue as to what this meant on the day of Pentecost, someone in the crowd accused these tongues-speaking 'charismatics' of being drunk. After all, this was the Harvest Festival, a time of merriment, rejoicing and joviality. Upon being unjustly accused, the Apostle Peter sprang to his feet in defense and defended the young Church when he said,

> These men are not drunk, as you suppose. It's only nine in the morning! No, this is what was spoken by the prophet Joel: In the last days, God says, I will pour out my Spirit upon all people. Your sons and daughters will prophesy, your young men will see visions, your old men will dream dreams. Even on my servants, both men and women, I will pour out my Spirit in those days, and they will prophesy (Acts 2:15-18).

Peter's rationale was that since it was only nine o'clock in the morning, these people could not possibly be drunk. There are several reasons why Peter could defend his co-believers in this way. First, the Jews did not drink wine unless they ate flesh, and they did not eat meat for breakfast; therefore they would not be drinking at this time.[10] The Jews knew this very well. Second, the hour of prayer was held at 9:00 a.m. An Israelite would not be reveling at that hour.[11] And third, the fast was not broken on the feast day until 10:00 a.m. Therefore, they would not be eating nor would they be drinking. The Jews were quite aware of this.[12] A possible fourth reason is that in all probability 'new wine' was not readily available at this season for this occasion.[13] And fifth, Peter took the helm as spokesman for the Church because he now had the power to do what he could not do previously. In his own strength he was a coward. But filled with the Holy Spirit, he was the person he was designed to be, meeting and filling divine destiny. Peter did not have to work hard to convince the onlookers. God had permitted the accusation of drunkenness against the believers to give the Apostle a reason and an opportunity to preach the good news to his audience resulting in their salvation.

Peter quoted Joel's prophecy given 830 years before Christ, indicating that the Promise had now been fulfilled. He took the Old Testament prophecy, "afterward, I will pour out my spirit on all people," and interpreted it to read, "*In the last days...I will pour out my Spirit on all people*" (cf. Joel 2:28 and Acts 2:17). Joel was speaking of the Messianic age beyond the restoration of the judgments he had just named. Peter said it had now been fulfilled.

Listen, dear reader, *it has been fulfilled*. You will see that this is the key to understanding why you may manifest the Spirit now. The early Church paid the price and waited for the gift of the Spirit. You and I need wait no longer. The

Spirit is here!

The Holy Spirit was given on that first Pentecost after Christ's resurrection and the result was that the believers spoke in tongues declaring "the wonders of God" (Acts 2:11). This is the Promise of the Father that Jesus had spoken of in Acts 1:4, 5. This outpouring in Acts 2 is acknowledged to be the baptism with the Holy Spirit by Bible-believing Christians everywhere.

Chapter Two

WHY DO THEY WAIT?

The Futility of Tarrying

One night following a service at Bethel Temple in Fresno, a leader of the church's jail ministry approached me and invited me to go with his team to the county jail to minister. I told him that I would be happy to accompany the group on my next trip to the area. This particular outreach leader had been in jail himself some time before for taking financial liberties while a manager with a fast food chain. It was then that he found the Lord. It so happened that a couple of weeks later I returned to Fresno and stayed with the pastor of the church. So I called the leader of the prison ministry and made arrangements to meet the group at the prison. At the appointed time the team captain picked me up and ten of us including a lively singing group headed for the prison. Upon entering the jail, the security guards logged us in and led us to the makeshift chapel. The musicians were tuning their guitars while the director was preparing the order of service. I was sitting in a chair looking over my sermon notes while we were waiting for the men to file out of their cells to join us.

In they came, about thirty of them, some with Bibles under their arms, and all sounding as if they were happy we had come. It was then that a prisoner with piercing black eyes, slicked-back hair, pointed his bony finger into my face as he advanced toward me. "That's the man! That's the man!" he exclaimed.

Rather startled, I asked, "What do you mean?"

He looked at the others who had gathered and, still pointing at me, blurted out, "That's the man!" Last night in my bunk I prayed that God would send someone to pray with me that I might receive the Holy Spirit." Pointing at me he said, "The Lord gave me a vision of you and told me you would help me. You're the man!"

I wondered if that's how Peter and Paul must have felt two-thousand years ago when Peter had his dream on the rooftop and Paul had a vision of a man from Macedonia standing and begging him to "...come over to Macedonia and help us" (Acts 16:8-10). I also remembered that Joel had said, "Your old men shall dream dreams, your young men shall see visions" (Joel 2:28).

We had a great service that night. The men sang with all their hearts. The team leader introduced me and I spoke for about twenty minutes on the need for the baptism with the Holy Spirit. "Ye will receive power when the Holy Spirit comes on you; and you will be my witnesses" (Acts 1:8).

When I gave the invitation, thirteen men responded by coming forward to receive the Holy Spirit. As they stood before me, each one spoke with tongues as we laid on hands—including the prisoner who had the vision.

Another prisoner sitting in his seat jumped up and burst out, "I just received the Holy Spirit!" He was shaking and speaking with tongues and praising God. We celebrated in the county jail that night as prophecy was being fulfilled, and visions and dreams became reality.

A History Lesson

You will remember that after his resurrection, Jesus remained on earth for forty days. He instructed His disciples regarding the direction their lives would take from this point forward. There would now be a closer relationship between Himself and His followers.

After the resurrection He promised to return to them in the Person of the Spirit to dwell in their hearts. He said,

> I will ask the Father, and He will give you another counselor to be with you forever—the Spirit of truth. The world cannot accept him because it neither sees him nor knows him. But you know him, for he lives with you, and will be in you. I will not leave you as orphans; I will cone to you (John 14:16-18).

Jesus emphasized that "He lives with you, and will be in you." The rationale of this text is that the Spirit lived with the early disciples at that time through the Person and bodily presence of Jesus. "For in Christ all the fullness of the Deity lives in bodily form" (Colossians 2:9); and "God was pleased to have all his fullness dwell in him" (Colossians 1:19).

When God came to earth to become man through the incarnation, we knew Him as the Person of Jesus Christ. He told His disciples that after He went away He would send another Counselor—the Holy Spirit. The coming of the Spirit, the Counselor, would take place after His death, resurrection and ascension, His glorification.

The Holy Spirit would live in the hearts of believers, which would bring Him into a closer relationship with them. He would not be limited to time and space any longer. This was all to occur on that first Pentecost.

Let us focus on Luke 24:44-53, and Acts 1:1-8 to understand more about what took place during the forty day period between the resurrection and ascension. Luke records:

> This is what I told you while I was still with you: Everything must be fulfilled that is written about me in the Law of Moses, the Prophets and the Psalms (Luke 24:44).

Then He opened their minds so they could understand the Scriptures. This is what is written: "The Christ will suffer and rise from the dead on the third day, and repentance and forgiveness of sins will be preached in his name to all nations, beginning at Jerusalem. You are witnesses of these things. I am going to send you what my Father has promised; but stay in the city until you have been clothed with power from on high."

When he had led them out to the vicinity of Bethany, he lifted up his hands and blessed them. While he was blessing them, he left them, and was taken up into heaven. They worshipped him and returned to Jerusalem with great joy, and stayed continually at the temple, praising God. We read in Acts 1:1-8:

> In my former book, Theophilus, I wrote about all that Jesus began to do and to teach until the day he was taken up to heaven, after giving instructions [concerning] the Holy Spirit to the apostles he had chosen.

After his suffering, he showed himself to these men and gave many convincing proofs that he was alive. He appeared to them over a period of forty days and spoke about the kingdom of God.

On one occasion, while he was eating with them, he gave them this command: "Do not leave Jerusalem, but wait for the gift my Father promised, which you have heard me speak about. For John baptized with water, but in a few days you will be baptized with the Holy Spirit."

So when they met together, they asked him, "Lord are you at this time going to restore the kingdom to Israel?" He said to them, "It is not for you to know the times or dates the father has set by his own authority. But you will receive power when the Holy Spirit comes on you; and you will be my witnesses in Jerusalem, and in Judea and Samaria, and to the ends of the earth."

Richard N. Longnecker, the Biblical commentator, notes,
> Apparently Luke also wanted to show through the word order of [Acts] verse 2 that Jesus' mandate to witness was given to the apostles, who acted through the Holy Spirit, whose coming was a direct result of our Lord's ascension. Each of the four factors, the witness mandate, the apostles, the Holy Spirit and the ascended Lord is a major emphasis that runs through the Book of Acts. [14]

From these passages we can clearly see the various instructions and mandates Jesus gave to his disciples before He ascended to the Father[15]. Let us look closely at the instructions Christ gave. These dealt with:

1. The validation and nature of His Messiahship (Luke 24:46).
2. The interpretation of the Old Testament from the perspective of the resurrection (Luke 24:44).
3. The responsibility of the disciples to bear witness to what had happened to them in regard to Israel's hope (Luke 24:48).
4. The power given to carry out the mandate to witness to the resurrection (Acts 1:8).
5. The witness to the convincing of 'infallible proofs' of the resurrection (Acts 1:3).
6. The witness to the Kingdom of God, Israel's hope, which would now be seen to be located in the hearts of believers (Acts 1:3).

Now let us look closely at the particular mandates:

1. Repentance should be preached for the remission of sins (Luke 24:47).
2. The disciples must be witnesses (Luke 24:4 cf. Acts 1:5).
3. They are promised power to witness (Acts 1:8).
4. They must wait for the clothing power (Luke 24:49).

This latter mandate was fulfilled at Pentecost and thus the first three mandates were enabled at the same time. Now, that the Holy Spirit is here, every believer can and should experience his own personal Pentecost when he comes to Jesus. Witnessing and propagating the Gospel should be a natural outflow of being clothed with the Holy Spirit power.

Many believe that 'tarrying' is still a command for us today, and that we must wait and pray for an untold number of hours, days, or even years to receive the Spirit. They think that Jesus' command to "stay [tarry] in the city [of Jerusalem], until you have been clothed with power from on high" (Luke 24:49) is still a commandment for all believers. They have not realized that the command was fulfilled at Pentecost. This was an error of many in the traditional Pentecostal movement in the early part of the twentieth century. Perhaps we did not know better in those days. But with sound exegetical skills we have come a long way in our understanding as to how our Lord intended us to be filled with the Spirit. Indeed, many in the Charismatic Renewal movement have helped to clarify this process.

'Tarrying' makes no sense once we realize that the Holy Spirit was given once at Pentecost and has been here with us ever since. Let me repeat, before Pentecost they had to wait or 'tarry' for up to that time the Holy Spirit had not been given, since Jesus had not yet been glorified" (John 7:39).

Please understand that today and ever since Pentecost,

Christ has been glorified! There is no longer a biblical mandate to wait. On Pentecost the manifestation of wind and fire signified that Christ had been received into heaven. His sacrifice had been accepted; He had received the Spirit from the Father and had poured out the Holy Spirit on His people!

To the New Testament Jews who understood Hebrew theology, Jesus is understood to be the High Priest who offered the sacrifice of His own blood on the Day of Atonement.[16] No longer would animal sacrifices—which were symbolic of the coming Christ—be needed to atone for our sins. Christ as High Priest was the permanent and eternal sacrifice for our sins. On this particular Yom Kippur, or Day of Atonement, we see the eternal High Priest who enters into the holy place 'not made with hands,' viz., into heaven itself, and has now appeared before God Almighty—once and for all—giving Himself as the everlasting sacrifice for the removal of sin. [17]

So why today do we have so many spending untold, agonizing, tearful hours in 'tarrying' meetings for the purpose of waiting and longing for God to fill them, or baptize them with the Spirit? Why do we wait?

The fact is, the gift of the Spirit is just that—a gift. A person cannot earn it, she cannot work for it, nor can she twist God's arm to do something that God has already done. One only needs to act in childlike faith to receive the gift that awaits her.

Since manifesting the Spirit is a verbal gift, it follows that one must willingly and volitionally accept it and use it to 'have' it. One must simply speak out in faith. God will not coerce a person to manifest the gift. He will not go against the wishes of His beloved. He is a Gentleman. He is patient.

Moreover, emotional jolts or physical manifestations are no proof that one has received the gift. Rather, in prayer and praise, one must utilize one's own power of speech, one's own vocal abilities, and speak forth in faith. "The spirits of prophets are subject to the control of prophets" (I Corinthians 14:32). That is man's part in the transaction. God invites our cooperation in the event.

As I pointed out in the last chapter, there are two equally good biblical terms used to describe this gift: one is to say, "Receive the Holy Spirit," the other is to say, "Manifest the Spirit." Truly, a person "receives the Spirit" when he accepts Jesus as Lord, as we have discussed. He manifests the Spirit, however, when in faith he opens his mouth and prays in the Spirit [tongues]. It is a faith proposition and a faith operation.

Some believers feel that they must attain perfection or holiness of character before God will accept them and fill them. This poses a difficulty, for it is an impossible task. We will never be perfect and any holiness we ever attain is God's, not ours. Some have put themselves through hours of horrendous introspection, agonizing before the Lord, trying to make themselves acceptable to God. Any psychologist can tell you that there is no end to introspection, self-recrimination and self-discovery. While it may be useful to do at times, it will not make you any 'better,' holy, or acceptable.

Looking within trying to find good in their hearts, (and finding very little), many believers begin to accrue guilt, which can finally lead to despair. The prophet said, "The heart is deceitful above all things and beyond cure. Who can understand it?" (Jeremiah 17:9).

Let's not waste our time trying to pull ourselves up by our own bootstraps. It can't be done. Any good that we are ever going to be or have emanates from God Almighty anyway. He gives us what makes us pleasing to Him. It is His righteousness that covers our guilt and sin—not ours.

Let me also say as an aside that Pentecost is not Yom Kippur, the Day of Atonement, which was the day for soul-searching and making atonement for the sins of the previous year. Pentecost was a harvest festival—a time of rejoicing and thanksgiving for the crops and provisions for another year. This was a time of celebration. We must remember that God accepts us where He finds us—in any condition—and then saves and fills us with His Spirit. From the time of our conversion to our Holy Spirit baptism, it is His job to clean us up so we can live for God. It cannot be otherwise.

Donald Gee, the well-known Pentecostal scholar, has said, "The immediate divine purpose of Pentecost was power, not holiness. Holiness by faith came before, and holiness by obedience had to follow after." [18]

We must come to grips with the reality of our nature. We are sinners by birth and sinners by choice. We must accept ourselves for what we are and believe that God accepts us for what we are. Holiness by obedience follows. He empowers us for that—we must merely cooperate.

Now let us turn our attention to the ensuing occurrences of the outpourings of the Holy Spirit in the Book of Acts beginning with the Gentiles.

Chapter Three

CORNELIUS AND THE ELECTRONICS ENGINEER

Does Everyone Speak in Tongues?

Sam Tong is an electronics engineer. He was involved in Scientology when I met him at our seminar on the Holy Spirit. Sam was hungry for God and in an honest search for truth. Because of his involvement in the cult, however, well-meaning Christians had told him that he could not receive the Holy Spirit. Obviously he had sinned against Christ and the Church. The poor man was disheartened and confused.

That night I told the story of the military Gentile Cornelius and Sam perked up. I mentioned that Cornelius simply believed Peter's message of salvation by faith, and that his faith touched God while Peter was speaking. God honored his faith by pouring out the Spirit upon him and the gathering of Gentiles present.

Sam took hold of this and regained hope. He immediately believed and accepted Jesus and received a glorious baptism with the Spirit. Later he told me, "When you said that Cornelius simply believed God, and that his faith went up as Peter preached, and God honored his faith, I began to tingle all over. I believe I was born again." He then began to speak with tongues as the Gentiles with Cornelius did.

Do All Speak With Tongues? - A Historical Vignette

In Acts 10 we note the appearance of *glossolalia* (speaking in tongues) when the Gentile received the baptism with the Spirit. Cornelius, a Godly Roman centurion, had an angelic visitation while in prayer. The angel told him to send for Peter who was in Joppa. Cornelius sent two servants and a soldier to Peter to persuade the latter to meet him at his quarters in Caesarea by the sea.

About the same time down in Joppa Peter had a 'visitation' from the Lord while praying on his housetop. He was hungry and was awaiting a meal. He fell into a trance and saw what appeared to be a large sheet let down from heaven. It was full of animals, birds and reptiles, 'clean' and 'unclean,' according to the Mosaic code. He heard a voice saying, "Get up, Peter. Kill and eat" (10:13).

Peter naturally refused, saying that he had never eaten anything common or unclean (v. 14). As a devout Jew, he had always kept the Mosaic laws regarding eating and drinking. The Spirit told him that he was not to call anything 'unclean' that God had cleansed. This happened three times after which the sheet was taken back up into heaven.

Peter was contemplating the vision when Cornelius' messengers arrived and called for him. The Spirit told Peter to go with them without hesitation. The men spent the night with Peter in Joppa, and the following day Peter accompanied the men to Caesarea.

When Peter met Cornelius, he inquired as to the reason for the invitation to Caesarea. Cornelius told him of his own angelic visitation and that the Lord had directed him to send for the apostle. Then he said, "Now we are all here in the presence of God to listen to everything the Lord has commanded you to tell us" (Acts 10:33).

Peter quickly understood God's revelation to himself in

Joppa during the holy visitation. The Gentiles were no longer to be considered 'unclean' by the Jewish Church. All men were equal before God. From this point Peter saw his task to be that of preaching the Good News to the Gentiles.

Peter preached to the group and while he was speaking, the Centurion, with his family and friends, believed the message of Jesus Christ. God poured out the Spirit upon them in response to their faith and they spoke in tongues. Luke declared in Acts 10:44-47:

> While Peter was still speaking these words, the Holy Spirit came on all who heard the message. The circumcised believers who had come with Peter were astonished that the gift of the Holy Spirit had been poured out even on the Gentiles. For they heard them speaking in tongues and praising God.

Then Peter said "Can anyone keep these people from being baptized with water? They have received the Holy Spirit just as we have." So he ordered that they be baptized in the name of Jesus Christ.

The pattern of receiving the Pentecostal experience accompanied with tongues that we saw in Acts chapter 2, is now repeated as the Holy Spirit is given to the Gentiles. Again, the observable, objective, uniform experience, the baptism with the Holy Spirit is demonstrated and the 'tongues' phenomenon exhibited.

When Peter returned to Jerusalem, the Jews questioned him about the matter of going into the home of a Gentile. The Christian brothers felt he had acted alone and without advice and consent of the group. His action was unusual for a Jew, as the rule was to seek consensus and guidance of the body in such matters before eating.

Moreover, the Gentiles did not observe the Mosaic laws concerning clean and unclean food, and they continually violated Jewish regulations concerning its preparation.

Therefore, the Jews did not eat with the Gentiles.

Peter defended his mission and actions before the Jewish believers by relating his own vision and visitation from the Lord. He said,

> As I began to speak, the Holy Spirit came on [the Gentiles] as he had come on us at the beginning [i.e., Pentecost]. Then I remembered what the Lord had said, "John baptized with water, but you will be baptized with the Holy Spirit." So if God gave them the same gift as he gave us, who believed in the Lord Jesus Christ, who was I to think that I could oppose God? (Acts 11:15-17).

This was proof positive to the Jewish Church that God had accepted the Gentiles, for they had received the same Gift, that the Jews had at Pentecost. The Jerusalem council confirmed Peter's action and objected no more. They declared, "So then, God has even granted the Gentiles repentance unto life" (Acts 11:18).

We must emphasize that *it was the speaking with tongues that carried the argument that day before the Jerusalem council.* This was how the Jewish Christians knew that God had accepted the Gentiles into His Body, the Church.

The wall of hostility between Jew and Gentile had been demolished and Jew and Gentile had now become one Body in Christ (Ephesians 2:14-17). This is the historical account as to how the Gentiles were accepted by God and the Jews and became part of the Body of Christ, the Church. Without this major historical account, you and I would not be worshipping Christians today. *Speaking with tongues was then, as it is now, the outward evidence or manifestation of the inward baptism with the Holy Spirit.* This is the thesis of this book.

God will accept anyone in whatever condition He finds him. If we put our trust in Him, and believe the message, He accepts us as is. Discipleship follows conversion, as does the filling of the Spirit. Let us be clear: 'tongues' is not the baptism with the Spirit. Rather, it is the *manifestation* of that baptism. A better reading of Acts 2:4 is, "They were all filled with the Holy Spirit, *after which* they began to speak in other languages, as the Spirit gave them ability."[19]

The Ephesians and the Holy Spirit

Now we change location, time and people, and see this pattern of baptism and tongues repeat itself in a different setting. Refer to Acts 19:1-6 to find the Holy Spirit being poured out on the disciples of John the Baptist. But, before we explore this text further, let us examine its background carefully for a proper reading and interpretation. A principle concern is the word, "disciples," which must be understood in its context. The text reads:

> While Apollos was at Corinth, Paul took the road through the interior and arrived at Ephesus. There he found some disciples and asked them, "Did you receive the Holy Spirit when you believed?" They answered, "No, we have not even heard that there is a Holy Spirit." [The Western text reads, "No, we have not heard whether any are receiving the Holy Spirit" (19:2).]

The Jews have always known of the Holy Spirit. Moses spoke of Him; the prophets spoke of Him, and John the Baptist had spoken of Him. Being John's disciples, they knew of the Holy Spirit. They only did not know that He had come. So Paul asked, "Then what baptism did you receive?"

"John's baptism," They replied. Paul said, "John's baptism was a baptism of repentance. He told the people to believe in the one coming after him, that is, in Jesus."

On hearing this, they were baptized in the name of the

Lord Jesus. When Paul placed his hands on them, the Holy Spirit came on them, and they spoke in tongues and prophesied. There were about twelve men in all (Acts 19:1-7).

Paul did not ask these Ephesian seekers to 'tarry' or to wait for a period of time to manifest the Spirit. Rather, he laid hands on them immediately and they then and there manifested the Spirit. They were baptized with the Holy Spirit. They spoke in tongues.

Some scholars[20] argue the case that the Ephesians were disciples of Jesus and that Paul was speaking to them about the manifestation of the Holy Spirit. This can hardly be so in the light of Chapter 19:3 where they declare themselves to be disciples of John the Baptist. They had received John's baptism. They had not yet been introduced to Jesus.[21]

Word studies do not disprove the point of Spirit baptism. John R. W. Stott said that the word 'baptism' is used seven times in the New Testament and in each case it refers to Christ's baptism of the disciple. He stresses the meaning of a baptism by the Holy Spirit into the body of Christ that I referred to in Chapter One when I explained three different meanings of 'baptism.' Stott would equate the 'baptism in the Holy Spirit' with the 'baptism into the Body of Christ.' However, a thorough reading does not indicate that these meanings of 'baptism' are the same.[22] I do not believe the meanings are equivalent because it is not congruent with the Ephesians' own statement. Most great leaders of the time had 'disciples.' The term is not unique to the Christian faith. Buddha, Confucius, Lao-Tse, and many rabbis had disciples. Gurus today have disciples. We should not assume, therefore, that the Ephesians were Christians simply because Acts 19:1 uses the term *mathetes* (disciple).

It is untenable and doctrinally incorrect to assert that the Ephesians were already Christians who were devoid of the Spirit when Paul met them. Paul states the case to be otherwise, for he says, "If anyone does not have the Spirit of

Christ, he does not belong to Christ" (Romans 8:9).

Acts 19:2 in the King James Version is not the best: "Have ye received the Holy Ghost *since ye believed?*" (Italics mine). Believing in Christ as Savior at conversion would itself invite the Holy Spirit into one's heart and life. The individual would already have the Spirit. A better reading is, "Have you received the Holy Spirit having believed," or, "when you believed?"

These people were not yet Christian; consequently they had not received the Spirit. Having been baptized by John, this group did not know that the Spirit (of Christ) had been dispensed. That is what this discussion is about.

Pentecostals have often cited the King James Version of this text to prove the doctrine of the baptism with the Spirit as a second work of grace. This terminology has been used to support a second—even a third—blessing theology, which some Pentecostals and Charismatics affirm. However, a close reading of this text does not support this doctrinal tenet.

Historically some Pentecostals and Holiness people have believed that 'getting saved' was (or is) the first blessing. They then pray for a 'second blessing,' a holiness experience, generally an emotional episode, in which they think their Adamic nature has been purged. The third blessing has been misinterpreted to be one of manifesting the Spirit, or to speak in tongues.

The fact is that there are many blessings for the Spirit-filled believer. G. Campbell Morgan, one of the most famous Bible expositors of his generation, said, "This was not a second blessing, but the first blessing, as the baptism and reception of the Holy Spirit always is."[23]

As noted, the Ephesians declared themselves to be disciples of John the Baptist in Acts 19:3.[24] Let us go over this crucial passage of Scripture again. Paul met the disciples of John when he returned to Ephesus from one of his missionary journeys and inquired as to their reception of the Spirit. He asked them, "Did you receive the Spirit having believed?" This is the literal rendering of the Greek text. It can also be translated to read, "Did you receive the Holy Spirit when you believed?"

This question was asked relative to their salvation. A paraphrase would be, "Have you received Christ, and therefore, received the Spirit?" The verb is used in the same tense and denotes a simultaneous act: believe-receive.

Note that Paul did not ask these people whether they had manifested the tongues experience. He did not ask them if they had received the baptism with the Holy Spirit. Paul was not speaking to Christians, for he above all people knew that Christians had received the Spirit by definition. Let us compare other Scriptures that support this interpretation.

Peter said in his Pentecostal sermon,

> Repent and be baptized, every one of you, in the name of Jesus Christ so that your sins may be forgiven. And you will receive the gift of the Holy Spirit (Acts 2:38).

Paul said, "If anyone does not have the Spirit of Christ, he does not belong to Christ" (Romans 8:9); and, "Do you not know that your body is a temple of the Holy Spirit, who is in you, whom you have received from God?" (I Corinthians 6:19).

Luke records in Acts 10:44: "While Peter was still speaking these words, the Holy Spirit came on all who heard the message." So we must understand and accept the fact that all believers, of any and all Christian churches, receive the Spirit when they accept Jesus.

Surely John the Baptist, the forerunner of Jesus, had prepared the way. His disciples knew that Messiah was to come, for John had taught them. Perhaps the same may be said of Apollos, who was eloquent and learned in the Scriptures. But Apollos echoed the message of John, his mentor. He knew only the teaching and baptism of John. Aquila and Priscilla "invited him to their home, and explained to him the way of God more adequately" (Acts 18:26).

This group of the Baptist's disciples did not know that the Spirit had come, and that He now dwelled in the hearts and minds of His people. But they were ready to accept and believe Paul's message when he encountered them and instructed them.

Properly understood, this text substantiates our view that people who accepted Christ in the New Testament period spoke with tongues at the time they became Christians, or invited Jesus into their hearts and were converted. It was the common and expected practice. It is my contention that this should be the normal spiritual experience for new converts today.

This is not to say, as some Pentecostal groups affirm, that a person must speak with tongues in order to be saved. We are not saying this. Experience and Scripture dictate otherwise. Rather, we affirm that any Christian may enjoy the experience and readily speak with tongues, or 'pray in the Spirit,' if he or she so desires. The believer has options as to how to pray.

> So what shall I do? I will pray with my spirit, but
> I will also pray with my mind; I will sing with
> my spirit, but I will also sing with my mind
> (I Corinthians 14:15).

Some Pentecostals insist that praying in the Spirit signifies ardent, laborious, or intercessory prayer. But this would not be consistent with the Corinthian passage. In the context of I Corinthians 14:15, 'praying in the Spirit' connotes praying in tongues. This is what the chapter addresses.

Please do not misunderstand me. Praying in the Spirit may be useful and at times necessary for ardent, laborious prayer and intercession. But in this context Paul is instructing the Church how to pray in their private prayer lives. Paul goes on to say that there are two ways of praying, with the mind (intelligence) and with the spirit (tongues). We can draw on both forms of prayer to enhance our spirituality.

For some issues we know how to pray, for others we may not know, hence we can pray in tongues (Romans 8:26, 27). "I will pray with my spirit" denotes determination and volition. One could decide to speak or sing with the Spirit and when one wished to do so. This applies to us today.

Paul commands believers to "pray in the Spirit on all occasions with all kinds of prayers and requests" (Ephesians 6:18). This is a command. Jude also commands us to "pray in the Holy Spirit" (Jude 20). Both of these Scriptures refer to praying in tongues.

The Jews (Acts 2), Cornelius' household (Acts 10), and the Ephesians (Acts 19) had similar experiences when they accepted Christ. They received the Holy Spirit and manifested His presence by speaking in tongues. The New Testament pattern, or paradigm, was clearly established. We must encourage believers to desire the manifestation of the Spirit, which they received when they came to Jesus.

It is my contention that all of God's people could and can speak with tongues "the wonders of God" (Acts 2:11), and "praising God" (Acts 10:46) if they know and accept the gift as a normal and expected part of Christian experience—*and if they so desire.*

The question arises in Christian circles as to whether a person *must* speak with tongues to manifest the Spirit. The answer is not that he/she *must*, but, as the noted Charismatic scholar and evangelist, Harold Bredesen, puts it, "He *gets* to" (emphasis mine). And to keep within the historical pattern, he *should*. It is the objective, uniform, observable and initial physical evidence that one has received the Gift.

The Samaritans and the Spirit

The experience in Acts 8 is singular and unique in relation to those of Acts 2, 10, and 19, which make up the New Testament model in regard to the 'tongues' issue. Please consider Acts 8:14-17 with me:

> When the apostles in Jerusalem heard that Samaria had accepted the word of God, they sent Peter and John to them. When they arrived, they prayed for them that they might receive the Holy Spirit, because the Holy Spirit had not yet come upon any of them; they had simply been baptized into the name of the Lord Jesus. Then Peter and John placed their hands on them, and they received the Holy Spirit.

The Samaritans did not initially manifest the Holy Spirit when they accepted Christ at Philip's preaching. "The Holy Spirit had not yet come upon any of them" (Acts 8:16). We note, however, the urgency and desire of the early Church to see to it that the believers manifested the Spirit without delay. They quickly sent the apostles, Peter and John, to Samaria to confer the Spirit. They were not content to let these converts remain without this blessing.

To believe that because 'tongues' is not mentioned in this chapter—so they must not have spoken in tongues—is to argue from silence. This is not 'proof' that they did not speak in tongues nor is it proof of anything else. Nor is it philosophically or logically a sound deduction. The paradigm has been established in the three texts cited above.

Let us take a moment to review what some of the great preachers, scholars and writers have had to say about the Samaritan revival and speaking in tongues referred to in Acts 8. Carl Brumback, the noted Pentecostal author, quotes some noted scholars on this text.[25]

Adam Clarke (1762-1832) a Methodist writer says, "It was the miraculous gifts of the Spirit which were thus communicated; the speaking with different tongues, and these extraordinary qualifications which were necessary for the successful preaching of the gospel."

Joseph Benson (1748-1821) another Methodist, scholar and preacher: "These new converts spake with tongues, and performed other extraordinary works."

Charles John Ellicott, an Episcopalian writer: "'When Simon saw that through the laying of the apostles' hands...' The words imply that the result was something visible and conspicuous. A change was wrought and men spoke with tongues and prophesied."

D. D. Whedon (1808-1888) a well-known expositor says, "Miniature Pentecost—same Charismatic effusions."

Alexander Maclaren, the noted Baptist minister writes: "The Samaritans had been baptized but still they lacked the gift of the Spirit."

J. S. Exell, Coeditor Pulpit Commentary: "This shows that the recipients of the Holy Ghost must in some external fashion—probably through speaking with tongues or working miracles—have indicated their possession of the heavenly gift."

I draw on these well-known authors, preachers and scholars to reiterate the cardinal truth that the baptism with the Holy Spirit is the reception of the Spirit, which manifests itself in speaking with tongues. Speaking in tongues is the outward manifestation of the inward experience of the Spirit.

Please bear with me and allow me to lead us on a little exploration of Acts 8, verses 14 and 17. While it may seem a bit tedious in the short-run, I think you will see that in the long run our exercise will prove to be enlightening. I repeat the text to make for easy consideration:

> When the apostles in Jerusalem heard that Samaria had *accepted* the word of God, they sent Peter and John to them. (emphasis mine) When

they arrived, they prayed for them that they might receive the Holy Spirit, because the Holy Spirit had not yet come upon any of them; they had simply been baptized into the name of the Lord Jesus. Then Peter and John placed their hands on them, and they *received* the Holy Spirit. (emphasis mine)

Two different words are used in this text. They are both translated 'receive' but they carry different meanings. They are the Greek words, *dedektai* (8:14), and *elambanon* (8:17). (These two words are the third person singular, perfect indicative of *dexomai*; and third person plural, imperfect active of *lambano*, respectively).

These two words have many and varied meanings and usages in Greek which we cannot fully explore in this work. Context must guide us here. Suffice it to say that *dexomai* carries the meaning 'to receive into and retain,' or 'contain.'[26] In our context this denotes a subjective experience. Apparently the translators in the New International Version recognized the difficulty and interpreted 'receive' (AV) in verse 8:14 to be 'accepted.' Thus, the text reads: "When the apostles in Jerusalem heard that Samaria had *accepted* the word of God..." (emphasis mine).

Lambano (8:17) talks about the *action* that is necessary on the part of the believer. "Dr. Hort...holds that the reception of the Holy Spirit is here [8:17] explained as in [Acts] 10:44 by reference to the manifestation of the gift of tongues...and he therefore renders it that they 'showed a succession of signs of the Spirit.'"[27]

Dedektai (v. 14) denotes an inner reception of the Spirit, while *elambanon* (v. 17) denotes an outward expression. Yet in the English texts both are translated 'receive.'

The Samaritans had *dedektai* (received) Christ *inwardly* as Savior in Acts 8:14 and thus had become believers. They were baptized in water (believers' baptism) but they had not *elambanon* (received) Christ *outwardly*; i.e., they had not manifested His presence openly until the apostles came down from Jerusalem and laid on hands.

> Since the day of Pentecost, those who 'belong to Christ' (Romans 8:9) have the Holy Spirit. But the Spirit had not yet been made manifest to the Christians in Samaria by the usual signs. This deficiency was now graciously supplied.[28]

We could read it as follows: "Then they laid hands on them, and they [manifested] the Holy Spirit" (Acts 8:17).

Dr. Coleman Cox Phillips, Pastor Emeritus of the Cathedral of the Valley Four Square Church in Escondido, California, and a contributor to the *Spirit Filled Life Bible*, adds insight when he says,

> There are three prepositions to keep in mind: 'with,' 'in,' and 'upon.' The Holy Spirit is 'with' unbelievers to convict and lead them to Christ. He dwells 'in' believers (Romans 8:9). And he falls 'upon' believers to empower them for service.

The Samaritans had the indwelling Christ and had been baptized. Now the Holy Spirit manifested His presence in their lives.

Many churches today are in the position of the church in Samaria. They have received the Spirit inwardly, but have not manifested Him outwardly. We must play 'catch-up' in the Church world in our endeavor to bring Christians the knowledge of their full blessings in Christ.

When a Christian asks whether one must speak with tongues to manifest the Spirit, it appears that the individual may not wish to do so for some reason. In the current American social milieu many Christians actually do not desire spiritual gifts or manifestations. They appear to be happy with an anemic spiritual state—one that will not require too much effort or make too many demands.

Is there the possibility that they have a fear of being

identified with the Pentecostals because they have seen some of the abuses or unbalanced use of spiritual gifts in times past? Might it be that they are simply proud of their church denomination and wish to go along with its teachings and the status quo and not shake things up or get 'too spiritual'? However, if they looked around them they are likely to encounter a group of Charismatics associated with their church. The Charismatics would be the ones who seem 'extra-lively' and are living their Christianity to the hilt. They are the ones with a gleam in their eyes, a bounce in their steps and purpose in their lives.

The question properly put is, "Do I have the privilege of speaking with tongues as they did in the New Testament? The answer is, "Of course, you do."

Some scholars and theologians who are predisposed against speaking in tongues have veered off into a type of dispensationalism in which they relegate miracles and spiritual gifts to the first century alone. They teach this to their students and churchmen, and by so doing inadvertently spawn unbelief in the church.

Carl Brumback defines dispensationalism as thus: "A dispensation is a period of time marked off in the history of man in which God has dealt with him according to certain laws and regulations for that period."[29]

The point at issue is that many Evangelicals have not realized that the church of the twenty-first century, now the third millennium, is locked in to the same dispensation as the Church in Acts. We are still in the New Testament Church Age. This is the era of THE SPIRIT. This period will continue until Jesus comes again. So we cannot exclude, nor should we exclude, gifts, miracles, and tongues from our experience.

This being so, we affirm with Evangelical Christians that we are indeed in the New Testament era, the Church Age, or the dispensation of the Holy Spirit, and are part of the New Testament Church of the first century. Whether the first century or the third millennium, we are all part of the New Testament Age and the New Testament Church.

Therefore, we have the privileges, power and promises given to the early Church. We Christians should be spiritually minded and not be content to stay on the sidelines or the outer edge of what is possible in the Christian experience. We must not allow ourselves to be blinded to the potential of the Holy Spirit in our lives by being satisfied with less than God has ordained for us.

Some believe that the gifts of the Spirit have ceased. An incorrect understanding of I Corinthians 13:8 is often used to discount the phenomenon. "Tongues shall cease" (KJV), taken out of its context, is their slogan. It would make an interesting study in itself to explore why a portion of God's Kingdom hopes for less than all that is available, spiritually speaking.

But let us look more closely at the Corinthian passage. Let us close this loophole in thinking. Perhaps in so doing we may come to a clearer understanding of the truth and see the benefits of speaking in tongues.

Tongues, prophecy, and knowledge are not the subject in I Corinthians 13. Love is the theme. Love is not a gift of the Spirit. Rather, it is the fruit of the Spirit, which Christians must cultivate. Paul juxtaposes the gifts and love to express the eternal nature of love as opposed to the short duration of the gifts.

Paul stresses that to have the gifts and not to have love is a real possibility. To support this point he says,

> But where there are prophecies, they will cease; where there are tongues, they will be stilled; where there is knowledge, it will pass away. For we know in part and we prophesy in part, but when perfection comes, the imperfect disappears (I Corinthians 13:8-10).

Obviously, perfection has not yet come. Contrary to some churchmen's tenets, the reference is not to the Bible as "that which is perfect," though we certainly uphold the plenary inspiration of the Scriptures. Rather, the Perfect is Jesus Christ Himself (see I John 3:2). When He comes, the gifts will no longer be needed. They will have served their purposes in this life. But in eternity "these three remain: faith, hope and love. But the greatest of these is love" (I Corinthians 13:13).

God's children should desire all that God has for them in relation to the reception of the Spirit and His gifts. We do not speak with tongues because we *must*. Rather, we readily accept the gift so that we may "worship the father in Spirit and in truth" (John 4:23), and "declare the wonders of God in our own tongues" (Acts 2:11).

What is the baptism with the Holy Spirit? We reiterate that it is the reception of the Spirit, which manifests itself in the speaking with tongues. It is an encounter with Jesus Christ, the mighty Baptizer with the Holy Spirit.

Eight hundred and thirty years before Christ Joel prophesied (Joel 2:28) that the Spirit would be poured out on all people. This prophecy was renewed by John the Baptist, the forerunner of Jesus (Matthew 3:11), and has been fulfilled. All over the world believers today are being filled with the Spirit and speaking with tongues the wonderful works of God!

Chapter Four

FIRE IN THE PENTAGON

The Purpose of the Baptism of the Holy Spirit

The phone rang in my office at the U.S. Naval Station in San Diego. I picked up the receiver to hear the familiar voice of my friend and colleague, Chaplain Bob Warren. It had been several months since he received his baptism with the Spirit at Sandia Base in the Bachelor Officers' Quarters.

"Hello, Bob. What's up?" It was good to hear from him.

"Can you come to Washington, D.C., to speak at the Pentagon Prayer Breakfast?"

"Will I have orders from the Commanding Officer?"

"No orders. You're on your own, Stan. Take leave without pay and get out here. I want you to tell the Pentagon all about the Holy Spirit. If anyone can do it, you are the one. I have it all set up."

"Well, give me some time to pray about it." I was wondering about the advisability of the work I was leaving behind. But after some time in prayer and consideration, "The Spirit bade me go with them, nothing doubting" (Acts 11:12 KJV).

I called Bob and told him that I would indeed come for

the meeting. Then I prayed that God would grant divine favor in this endeavor, as this was a unique opportunity the Spirit was offering in a highly unlikely setting. The date was set and I was ready to go.

My wife, Verna, and daughter, Gena, and I arrived in Washington and stayed with Bob and his wife, Genece. The following morning we drove down to the Defense Department to meet those attending the breakfast. It was held in the executive dining area at the Bureau of Naval Personnel Annex.

Bob introduced me and after some greetings I took out my New Testament and spoke for twenty minutes on the baptism with the Holy Spirit. I emphasized that the manifestation of speaking with tongues was the initial physical evidence that one had received the Spirit.

I spoke briefly with the intention of dismissing them quickly due to their tight schedules. I concluded my talk by saying, "If we had the time and place, we could pray with those who desired to receive the Spirit and they could manifest His Presence by speaking in tongues in a matter of moments."

A voice from the third row spoke out. I looked to see a bemedaled Marine Fighter Pilot in full uniform addressing me. Looking me straight in the eyes, Major Myrl Allinder queried, "Why can't we do it now?"

Perhaps it was because we were in the Pentagon that I was a bit taken back by his pointed question. Nonetheless, I retorted, "The Spirit is here. We can indeed do it right now. Come on forward!"

The Marine officer and several other civil servants sprang forward, fell to their knees, raised their hands heavenward, and began to pray.

Commander Carl Wilgus, Bob Warren, and I laid hands on the Major and he prayed in tongues, as did the others. There was an outpouring of the Holy Spirit on the group as officers and civil servants spoke in tongues, praising and magnifying God—all before work began at 8:00 a.m.!

Several months later Major Allinder spoke for the Full Gospel Business Men's Fellowship, International Convention in Washington, D.C. He told this story.

> May 17th, 1968 is a red-letter day to me because on that date Jesus baptized me in His Holy Spirit. I know the date, the hour and the place, and I can show you the exact spot where I received!
>
> A Presbyterian Chaplain was there by the name of Bob Warren, a Nazarene Officer named Carl Wilgus, and an Assemblies of God minister, Stan Linzey. As the latter was speaking about the things of the Spirit, my soul began to burn within me and I cried out, "Sir, what is to prevent me from receiving this baptism that Jesus gives?"
>
> He replied that there wasn't a thing to prevent it. I got down on my knees and lifted up my hands to the Lord in complete surrender. Rev. Linzey, the Assemblies of God brother, laid his hands on the back of my head. My Presbyterian brother was on one side, my Nazarene brother on the other side, and I was the Baptist in the middle!
>
> I felt something like Roman candles burning inside of me, the flames leaping up as they went through my body, burning out all the dross, and I was filled to overflowing with the love of Jesus, literally crushed with the wonder of His tender love. I'd never known such love.

The Major continued to tell the story of how God had used him to testify for Christ following this experience and how he had witnessed for Christ in Vietnam. He said, "Because I am a fighter pilot, I understand physical power…but what I could not understand was my lack of spiritual power! Now I have it!"[30]

Myrl attained the rank of Colonel in the Marine Corp and since his retirement has founded and directs 'Til Shiloh Comes, Inc.,' an organization that trains young men in the basics of Christian warfare, ministering on the streets, in prisons, hospitals and nursing homes.

The Colonel wrote me on July 13, 1991 on the occasion of Verna's and my 50th wedding anniversary. Among the many good comments, he wrote:

> My first encounter with you, Stan, was on a Wednesday morning in May 1968 as the Holy Spirit programmed you to be a conductor of His power and presence into my life. I had struggled the whole previous 24 hours, up all night, with John 14, especially verses 12-14.
>
> My heart was terribly troubled, and my Christian walk was lacking in the life-changing power of Jesus to testify to others. I was ready to leave the Admiral's dining room at the Navy Annex at about 7:45 that morning (May 17, 1968) when a man I had never met nor seen before in my life—you! —stood and pointed in my direction and said, 'The Holy Spirit just told me to read you a Scripture.'
>
> I knew what the Scripture was going to be! I fell on my knees in fear and trembling as you read John 14, laid hands on me, and I received the baptism in the Holy Spirit and fire. My life, and the lives of my family, and of thousands of marines and sailors, soldiers and airmen, these lives were forever changed. The ripples of the impact of that moment still go out around the world.
>
> I just returned from South America, and am leaving shortly for Canada and then Egypt and

Africa, after helping 1,500 young people through 'boot camp' training to take the Gospel of Jesus Christ to the lost.

Ever since this Marine welcomed the Holy Spirit into his life, the power of God has flowed through him and he traverses the world ministering in Jesus' Name with the power that enables him to minister in a way that he never could before.

The question arises, "Is this spiritual power available to all Christians?" My answer is a resounding, "Yes!" These lives could not have been changed without it.

What Is The Purpose Of The Baptism With The Holy Spirit?

Some raise the question as to why a Christian should desire to speak with tongues. There are many reasons why God's people should desire this gift. I would like to share two basic reasons here why one should desire this unique experience. In the next chapter I will share more. For now let us consider these: (1) that he might have power for service, and (2) that he might be spiritually edified. Jesus said:

> But you will receive power when the Holy Spirit comes on you; and you will be my witnesses in Jerusalem, and in all Judea and Samaria, and to the ends of the earth (Acts 1:8).

Paul said in I Corinthians 14:4, "He who speaks in a tongue edifies himself."

Power for Service

The rationale for the baptism with the Spirit is that it gives power for service and builds one up in his own personal faith and spirit. The Holy Spirit enables the believer to witness more effectively for Jesus Christ. All believers need this power, for all have the commission to witness according to Matthew 28:19, 20:

> Therefore Go and make disciples of all nations, baptizing them in the name of the Father and of the Son and of the Holy Spirit, and teaching them to obey every thing I have commanded you. And surely I will be with you always, to the very end of the age.

The New Testament Church was a powerful Church and Christ intended that it continue as such. Jesus gave his disciples power when he commissioned them in Matthew 10:1, 7, and 8. He called his twelve disciples to him and gave them authority to drive out evil spirits and to cure every kind of disease and sickness.

As you go, preach this message: 'The kingdom of heaven is near.' Heal the sick, raise the dead, cleanse those who have leprosy. Drive out demons. Freely you have received, freely give.

The disciples did miraculous works because Christ empowered them to carry out ministry just as He had done. After His resurrection and ascension, He returned in the Person and power of the Holy Spirit to live in the hearts of believers and thus continue His works and carry on His ministry through them.

Prior to Pentecost the disciples had a delegated authority to perform miraculous ministry. That is, He appointed and entrusted them with His authority to represent Him and act in His name. Since Pentecost, believers have an inherent authority; that is, Christ now dwells in believers and performs His work through them and their activities. Jesus said,

> Go into all the world and preach the good news to all creation. Whoever believes and is baptized will be saved, but whoever does not believe will be condemned. And these signs will accompany those who believe: In my name they will drive out demons; they will speak in new tongues; they will pick up snakes with their hands; and when

> they drink deadly poison, it will not hurt them at
> all; they will place their hands on sick people,
> and they will get well (Mark 16:15-20).

Some scholars contend that Mark 16:9-20 is not in the original manuscripts. It is, however, in many of the ancient manuscripts and is congruent with the text in Matthew 10:1, 7, and 8.[31]

Not only did they do the marvelous works that Jesus did, but greater works followed after He returned to the Father. Perhaps by "greater works" Jesus meant more in number; for by the Spirit He would dwell in the hearts of His people worldwide and thus multiply Himself and His works. Jesus said in John 14:12,

> I tell you the truth, anyone who has faith in me
> will do what I have been doing. He will do even
> greater things than these, because I am going to
> the Father.

These mighty signs and wonders performed by Jesus on earth were multiplied over and over in the lives of the disciples. These signs attested to His claim to "all power" (Matthew 28:18), and signified the transfer of this power to the Church for the purpose of propagating the Good News.

Jesus Christ did not intend for His Church to be an anemic, fearful, powerless group of sheep moved by the whims of Satan or the world. Based on what we sometimes observe, we might be tempted to think that the postmodern Church is powerless and ineffective. Some might be tempted to consider the Church to be a non-entity or not a power to be reckoned with. It does not seem to bother anyone. Even worse, it does not seem to excite anyone. Probably worst of all, it sometimes seems that it does not save anyone. It does not seem to proclaim a strong Gospel, calling the lost to repentance and faith in Christ. It sometimes seems that it fails to be a vital witness for Jesus.

Christ intended for His Church to be a vital body with the resurrection power of His life force coursing through its veins. He meant it to be a fearless body, unafraid of demons or men. He meant it to be a powerful body with the Christ-given ability to save the lost, heal the sick and build the Kingdom of God.

In some locales churches have substituted programs of talent and entertainment in lieu of preaching of the Word, healing the sick, and setting the captive free from sin and sickness. The Church seems to have joined this world's system, whereas Jesus desired that it be otherworldly, standing apart from earthly powers to serve as Salt and Light. Jesus prayed His high priestly prayer in John 17:15, 16:

> My prayer is not that you take them out of the world but that you protect them from the evil one. They [the disciples, hence the church] are not of the world, even as I am not of it. Sanctify them by the truth; Your word is truth. As you sent me into the world, I have sent them into the world.

Christ sent them into the world to live for Him and to proclaim the Good News of the Kingdom of God. To accomplish this He said in Luke 10:19,

> I have given you authority to trample on snakes and scorpions, and to overcome all the power of the enemy; nothing will harm you.

Snakes and scorpions may typify demonic powers, while "the enemy" is Satan himself. Satan has been defeated by the Cross, and the Resurrection and the forces of light are pushing the forces of darkness. Jesus said, "I saw Satan fall like lightning from heaven" (Luke 10:18). Paul said in II Corinthians 10:3-5,

> For though we live in the world, we do not wage war as the world does. The weapons we fight with are not the weapons of the world. On the contrary, they have divine power to demolish

strongholds. We demolish arguments and every pretension that sets itself up against the knowledge of God, and we take captive every thought to make it obedient to Christ.

Concerning His Church, Jesus said in Matthew 16:18, "The gates of hades will not overcome it."

The meaning is not that evil powers shall not be able to attack and conquer the Church. To the contrary, evil forces shall not be able to stand against the onslaught of the Church *as she attacks them*! The Church is on the march against evil. Evil cannot withstand the Church militant! Satan or the hosts of darkness cannot defeat the Church. The Church cannot fail because the power of the Spirit keeps it alive and vital to the end. All the cosmic forces opposed to Christ and His Kingdom will finally fall, but His Kingdom shall have no end.

The New Testament Church was a power for God—a force to reckon with. She attacked the Roman Empire by preaching the Gospel, casting out demons, and healing the sick as Jesus said she would. Finally, she assaulted the imperial palace itself and made believers in Caesar's household (see Philippians 4:21).

At a dinner meeting some time ago I engaged in conversation with a bright young man concerning what he perceived to be the ineffectiveness of the modern Christian Church. He was a nominal churchman who had become disenchanted with his church. I had told him of people being converted in our ministry, and of some healings that had taken place. He became interested and wanted to probe deeper.

"May I ask you a personal question? He inquired.

"Certainly." I was curious as to what he might want to know.

"Have you personally seen miracles in answer to prayer, or healings in your own ministry?"

"I surely have." I explained, "God manifests His power

in miracles and healings on a regular basis in our meetings." Then I proceeded to share some of our experiences such as the following.

While conducting a Holy Spirit seminar one night, I announced that we would pray for the sick. At the appropriate moment in the service I invited the congregation forward for prayer and anointing with oil (see James 5:14, 15).

An elder pushed a wheelchair to me. In it sat a rather well dressed lady. She wheeled herself toward me to get closer. I bent forward and asked, "What is your sickness?"

"Rheumatoid arthritis," she replied. Stiff and rigid, she was in pain and could hardly move. "How long have you been in the wheel chair?"

"Ten years," she whispered.

"Are you telling me that you haven't walked in ten years?

"That's right," she nodded.

I said to the church elders, "Lift her out of the chair." They gently lifted her to her feet. She stood frozen for a few seconds facing the congregation. All eyes were on her. Then I commanded her, "In the Name of Jesus, walk!"

The congregation leaned forward attentively to see what would happen. Then it happened. Unsteady and hesitating at first, she took a couple of trial steps. Then she walked confidently across the church in front of the podium to the cheers and shouts of the people. She wept as she realized she was healed.

On seeing the paralytic walk, a young man sitting on the back pew, gripped by the Spirit and convicted of his own sinful state, jumped up and ran to the altar shouting, "God save me! God forgive me!" Then he added, "If God can heal this woman, He can save me!"

That night the lady walked out of the church a renewed and healed woman and the young man walked out saved! This is the purpose of miracles.

A few nights later the lady returned to church on her own strength and took a seat on the front row. During the praise service Jesus baptized her with the Holy Spirit and she began to speak in tongues "the wonderful works of God."

The man at the dinner table was deeply moved as I recounted these events. He said, "I've never heard anything like this." I suggested that he attend church where God's power is regularly and openly displayed. People abound in disbelief partially because they are not allowed to be privy to what the Spirit is doing in the world today.

Personal Edification

The second purpose for the baptism with the Spirit is that of personal edification. "He who speaks in a tongue edifies himself" (I Corinthians 14:4). To "edify oneself" means that a person can build himself up in faith and strengthen himself spiritually. Countless testimonies attest to this.

A vibrant middle-aged Mexican sister received her baptism with the Spirit one night when we laid hands on her. She easily and quietly spoke with tongues for some time. Two nights later she told me her story of spiritual victory.

Years previously someone tried to destroy her reputation and cruelly offended her by gossiping. This had caused her much longstanding bitterness and hatred toward the offender. That evening she said, "Brother Linzey, since I received the baptism with the Holy Spirit, God has taken the hate and bitterness out of my heart. I don't hate this person any more. I am forgiven. I am free!" She showed it too and she radiated great joy.

The word 'edification' may sound rather pious to twenty-first century minds. But it is not when one considers the Greek text. Arnold Bittlinger, the noted German theologian who delivered a series of Bible Studies at an Ecumenical Church Conference on 'Charismatic Church

Life,' says that what is meant here is the "constructive building up of the personality."[32]

W. J. Hollenweger, the noted Charismatic scholar, characterizes the tongues phenomenon as "the psycho-hygienic function of speaking in tongues."[33] He supports the notion that praying in tongues, or in the Spirit, tends to promote health, is cleansing psychologically and is in general emotionally beneficial. Speaking in tongues edifies the person.

There is a school of psychology that confirms the therapeutic effect of speaking with tongues. Morton Kelsey, an Anglican clergyman and psychotherapist writes, "There are people who without this experience [tongues] would never have been able to come to psychological maturity."[34]

The noted Lutheran Charismatic clergyman, Laurence Christensen wrote, "When somebody prays in tongues he is built up in that area of his life and person which is in greatest spiritual need."[35] This statement is verified by the Scripture that notes that the inner person is built up, or edified, when he prays in tongues (I Corinthians 14:4). Dr. Paul Tournier, the noted Swiss psychiatrist, penned the following:

> In [the New Testament] we read the wonderful dialogues through which Jesus transforms the lives of those whom he meets, drawing out the person buried beneath the personage, and revealing personal contact to them. We witness the growth of real community in the Early Church.
>
> Glossolalia, or speaking with tongues, which played such an important part then...appears to answer to the need of the Spirit *to express the inexpressible, to carry the dialogue with God beyond the narrow limits of clearly intelligible language*" (Italics mine).[36]

The Bible attests to this truth in I Corinthians 14:2,

Anyone who speaks in a tongue does not speak to men but to God. Indeed, no one understands him; he utters mysteries with his spirit.
In the same way, the Spirit helps us in our weakness. We do not know what we ought to pray, but the Spirit himself intercedes for us with groans that words cannot express. And he who searches our hearts knows the mind of the Spirit, because the Spirit intercedes for the saints in accordance with God's will (Romans 8:26, 27).

Dr. Lincoln Vivier, a physician in the University of Johannesburg, South Africa, wrote an interesting paper for his colleagues in the Department of Psychiatry. He had given psychological evaluations to a group of South African Pentecostals to ascertain their mental acumen and personality status. He wished to find out if they were 'normal' people in all respects. (Today, some people tend to think that the Pentecostals are suspect in these areas. This is unfortunate stereotype that caused many in the Charismatic Renewal to desire to disassociate with them.)

He reported that the people he tested were not only 'normal' in all respects, but that they were also better able to endure stress and strain than others who had not received the gift.[37] These plus other recent studies (e.g., Tournier, Kelsey, and others), contradict the prejudices and earlier negative views concerning the Pentecostals and their mental health. The baptism in the Spirit is also given as an aid in the believer's prayer life. Paul commands, "Pray in the Spirit on all occasions with all kinds of prayers and requests" (Ephesians 6:18). Jude said, "But you, dear friends, build yourself up in your most holy faith and pray in the Holy Spirit. Keep yourself in God's love..." (v. 20, 21).

Please note that Paul's statement to the Ephesians is given in the imperative mode in the Greek text. "Pray in the Spirit." This is a command. A command can only be given if there is the possibility of carrying it out; and we note this possibility according to Romans 8:26, 27, "...The Spirit himself intercedes for us with groans that words cannot express...{He} intercedes for the saints in accordance with God's will."

To carry out this command connotes the necessity of having been baptized with the Holy Spirit. He enables one to pray in the Spirit. Note that praying with the Spirit in I Corinthians 14 signifies praying with tongues. The Apostle Paul said in I Corinthians 14:15, "So what shall I do? I will pray with my spirit, but I will also pray with my mind; I will sing with my spirit, but I will also sing with my mind.

One person having been filled with the Spirit approached me at the close of one of our services and said, "Since I received the baptism with the Holy Spirit, I pray only in tongues now." She then asked, "Is this correct?"

I replied that this was not correct. In regard to praying with the Spirit (tongues) and praying with our understanding (our native language), it is not a matter of either-or, but rather it is a case of both-and. We are to pray in both modes. Tongues are given to enhance the total prayer life. Also, the Scripture cited indicates that a person can pray in tongues at will, as one does in one's own language.

It is common in many Evangelical churches to take prayer requests so that we may pray intelligently for people's needs. Thus we pray with the mind, that is, with the understanding. But we can also pray in greater depth in the Spirit when we pray in tongues. Paul indicated this in the Corinthian passage.

One reason for praying in tongues is that there are occasions in which we do not know how to pray. We do not always know the mind of God in every matter, and at times our motives may be mixed or uncertain. In this sense, praying in tongues would apply to the private prayer life. Praying publicly in tongues requires an interpretation and is done for different reasons, which we may discuss on another occasion.

Reverend Dutch Sheets, senior pastor of Springs Harvest Fellowship in Colorado Springs, Colorado, commenting on Romans 8:26, 27 writes,

> At times when I am praying in the Spirit I feel like a butterfly looks. They flutter this way and that, up and down, 'herky-jerky.' It appears they do not have the slightest idea where they are going. They almost look drunk. When I begin to pray in the Spirit, not knowing what I am saying, sometimes with my mind wandering this way and that, I feel as though I'm trying to move in the 'butterfly anointing.'
>
> But as surely as that butterfly knows exactly where it's going, so the Holy Spirit directs my prayers precisely! They WILL 'light upon' correctly.[38]

Selfishness may also creep into our prayers and desires. When one prays in the Spirit, however, she may rest assured that she prays in accord with the mind and will of God, for the Spirit assists her in her prayers. Jude writes in verses 20 and 21,

> But you, dear friends, build yourself up in your most holy faith and pray in the Holy Spirit. Keep yourself in God's love as you wait for the mercy of our Lord Jesus Christ to bring you to eternal life. Keep yourself in the love of God.

This indicates that one can keep himself in God's love by praying in the Spirit.

Michael Green suggests, "By prayer in the Holy Spirit it is sometimes suggested that prayer in tongues is indicated. If so, it is hinted at very obscurely."[39] But we note in our study thus far that on the occasions that the Holy Spirit has been manifested, the phenomenon of tongues was present. This is particularly so in the Book of Acts. By the Law of First Mention (see Acts 2:4), we learn that the term, 'baptize with the Holy Spirit' connotes speaking in tongues and will always carry this meaning. Also, it seems to indicate that one can keep himself in the sphere of God's love by so praying. Why wouldn't any child of God desire this?

To reiterate the question, "What is the purpose of the baptism with the Holy Spirit and speaking with tongues?" The answer is that there are many purposes, two of which are (1) that the Church might have power for service in carrying out the Great Commission, and (2) that the individual believer may be edified spiritually.

Chapter Five

IS SOMEONE'S LIFE AT STAKE?

Reasons to Speak in Tongues

In November 1990 Verna and I spent a couple of days relaxing at the Home of Peace, a missionary home in Oakland, California. There I met Dr. Sam Mings, an athlete and a Baptist businessman from Hurst, Texas.

Dr. Mings had been plagued with serious health problems that had seriously threatened his life. Through his pain, however, he had come into Christian fellowship, attended seminary and developed a strong relationship with the Lord. He became interested in winning athletes to Jesus Christ.

He founded 'Lay Witnesses for Christ, International' (LWFC), the largest ministry for Olympic athletes in the world. His organization has been effective in winning world-class sports figures to Christ such as Valerie Brisco, Greg Foster, Florence Griffith, Carl Lewis and Mark Anderson.

Carl Lewis won his fourth consecutive Olympics Gold Medal in 1996 in the long jump competition. Valerie Brisco ran the 200 and 400 meter run in 1984. Florence Griffith-Joyner won her gold medal running the 100 and the 200-meter run in 1988. Dr. Ming's testimony and those of Mark

Anderson, Carl Lewis and Greg Foster appeared in VOICE Magazine.[40]

I asked him, "Sam, have you ever given consideration to the baptism with the Holy Spirit, speaking with tongues?"

"Yes, sure. I am aware of it. Some of our group speak with tongues. But, it is like the other gifts, I suppose. God will give it to me if He wants me to have it."

"That's rather an apathetic attitude, isn't it, Sam?" I replied. "If God wants everyone in the world saved, He'll save them too, won't he?"

"I see your point," he said. I briefly explained the doctrine to him as found in Acts 2, 8, and 10. As a seminary graduate, Sam readily understood the theological implications of what I was saying.

"Sam," I said, "You already have the Spirit in that you are a Christian. I am not suggesting that you receive the Spirit again. And I am not implying that you have not been effective in your present ministry. You have a great ministry, and you have the fruit to show for it—athletes won to Christ. However, the ability to pray in the Spirit will enhance your ministry, making it even greater than it now is, perhaps greater than you can imagine."

Sam looked at me intently for a moment and said, "Stan, you have made more sense to me on this subject than many others who have spoken to me. Let's go to my room and pray."

"Fine with me," I said.

Seated in his room I said, "Sam, I'm going to lay my hands on you and pray. When I do, strange sounding syllables may come to your mind. Sam, if you are not inhibited…"

"I'm not inhibited!" he broke in.

"I am sure that you are not," I said. "Then, if you will speak out those syllables as they come to you, you will begin speaking in tongues in a matter of moments. Let's pray."

"Dear Lord," I prayed, "please baptize my brother with

the Holy Spirit." Sam began to whisper softly in tongues.

"Give it a voice, Sam," I urged. He did so and began speaking fluently. He had a wonderful experience with the Spirit.

Sam and I were co-speakers at David Ministries that evening in Hayward, California at the invitation of the Director, Reverend James C. Davis, Jr. That evening before the group Dr. Mings related the unique event that he had experienced in prayer that afternoon.

Here is what he said: "In seminary I wrote a paper on 'Why Tongues are not for Today.' I got an 'A' on the paper. But since having prayer with Stan this afternoon and manifesting the Spirit, I shall have to go home and tear up the paper."

Dr. Mings wrote me later: "God bless you for all your love and encouragement to me, my ministry and my spiritual well-being. Your approach and insight is anointed of God. I'll never forget you, and I covenant to pray for you daily. Thank you for spending time sharing and praying with me. It [November 9, 1990] was and shall always be a special time in my life."

More recently he wrote: "Since I've seen you, I've been to Mexico City where 2,500 came to Christ...then two Olympic Champions (Joe De Loach and Calvin Smith) accompanied me to New Zealand. Again, many were saved with much praising of the Lord."

CHARISMA (November 1991) carried the story of the World Track and Field Championships in Tokyo, Japan, in which Carl Lewis set a new world record when he ran 100 meters in 9.8 seconds. At that time Lewis said, "I did what I did through the grace and power of God."

Tadashi Nakagawa, secretary of the Full Gospel Business Men's Fellowship, International, Tokyo, wrote,

"We strongly felt that it [the championships] was the beginning of the Japanese revival. It was the first time

Christian ministries had been carried on front pages of Japanese newspapers."[41]

CHARISMA continued, "Sam Mings, founder of Lay Witnesses for Christ, didn't realize the full extent of this miracle until talking with other ministries back in the States. They said, "We've been trying to minister to Japan for years, and it's almost like it is in Europe: cold and indifferent," he commented.

"They've got their thing, and they're going to keep it Buddhist. Japan is a predominantly Buddhist nation where just one percent of 112 million people are Christian."

"Dr. Sam Mings and his lay witnesses could well be the spearhead to crack Japan and the rest of the world with the Gospel through his world-class athletes." Evidently God is enhancing His ministry!

What Does The Bible Say?

Why should I, or anyone else, desire to speak with tongues? What is the purpose of tongues in the life of the believer? Why must this be a problematic issue for the Church among Bible-believing Christians? Does it not often cause division among God's people? Let us touch briefly on some of these issues. At the end of the book questions such as these are treated more in depth.

Biblically speaking, tongues are the initial physical evidence that one has received the baptism with the Holy Spirit. The Book of Acts portrays this in chapters 2, 10, and 19. Also see my chapters one, two and three for discussion.

While tongues is not mentioned in Acts 8:14-17 as having occurred when Peter and John laid hands on the Samaritans, there was an observable manifestation which should be tongues' (according to pattern) for Simon the sorcerer wished to buy the gift. He saw something that he wanted and was willing to pay for it. His motive and greed were apparent, but the fact remains, he saw an observable spiritual event. For those wishing to argue that there is no proof here that the Samaritans spoke in tongues, the question may be asked, "What then was Simon wishing to purchase?" The enemy will pay money to duplicate God's gifts.

The Bible says, "Be filled with the Spirit" (Ephesians 5:18). This command is given to all Christians. R. A. Torrey points out that there are at least nine different phrases that are used in the New Testament to describe one and the same experience:

"Baptized with the Holy Spirit"
"Filled with the Holy Ghost"
"The Holy Ghost fell on them"
"The gift of the Holy Ghost was poured out"
"Receive the Holy Ghost"
"The Holy Ghost came on them"
"Gifts of the Holy Ghost"
"I send the promise of the Father upon you"
"Endued with power from on high"

Torrey says,

> All these expressions are used in the New Testament to describe one and the same experience. The baptism with the Holy Spirit...is a definite experience of which one may and ought to know whether he has received it or not. [42]

In all fairness the question may be asked, "Is not the fruit of the Spirit better evidence of being Spirit-filled than speaking with tongues?" Now, at first blush this sounds holy, pious, logical, and even plausible—maybe even desirable—to some. However, let's scrutinize this reasoning a little more closely.

When one initially comes to Christ, there has been no time to bear fruit. As one matures and develops Godly character, fruit should eventually be forthcoming. As one has had the opportunity to "grow in grace and in the knowledge of our Lord and Savior Jesus Christ" (II Peter 3:18), fruit will eventually be evident. Speaking in one's heavenly language indicates that one has received the blessing that initiated one's walk with Jesus. This is the first reason for speaking in tongues.

The second reason for speaking with tongues, as previously pointed out, is so that one may have power for service and to witness. Jesus gave the Great Commission in Mark 16:15-18, and Matthew 28:18-20. The disciples were to preach the Good News to all the world, and Jesus promised to go with them when He said, "Lo, I am with you always, even unto the end of the [age]." Mark said, "And they went forth, and preached everywhere, the Lord working with them, and confirming the word with signs following" (Mark 16:20).

Jesus gave the command not only to the twelve, or only to ministers and elders. He gave the Commission to all who would believe in Him throughout the New Testament Church age. This includes believers today.

The Church is to be a powerful body, able to make converts from those in the world, thwarting Satan's attacks, and exalting Jesus Christ. Paul made converts in the palace at Rome. He wrote in the Philippian letter (4:22): "All the saints salute you, chiefly they that are of Caesar's household."

Peter and John healed the lame man at the Beautiful Gate of the Temple (Acts 3). Philip, the deacon, preached the great revival in Samaria (Acts 8). It appears that the entire city (area) was converted by one layman's preaching, and signs and wonders accompanied the revival. These experiences have been repeated time and again through two thousand years of Church history, as vibrant Spirit-filled men and women have given themselves fully to follow Jesus.

A third reason for speaking in tongues is that it aids in the development of the personality. We have addressed this issue as well, but it bears reiterating. "He who speaks in a tongue edifies himself" (I Corinthians 14:4).

Walter Hollenweger describes this as the "constructive building up of the personality"[43] He says that a person needs a nonintellectual means of meditation and release. He quotes Friedrich Heiler, German theologian and leader of the German High Church Union, who feels that this "pouring out of one's heart to God has the effect of an inner release that goes beyond the contribution of psychoanalysis."[44]

On I Corinthians 14:4 the NIV Study Bible footnote reads: "This edification does not involve the mind since the speaker does not understand what he has said. It is a personal edification in the area of the emotions, a deepening conviction of fuller commitment and greater love."[45]

A fourth reason to pray in tongues is the enhancement of the prayer life. We do not always know how to pray as we ought (Romans 8:26). Our prayer life can become cold and formal if we do not monitor it carefully. It does not take long to pray for the things we need, or want, or for family and friends. So we may cease prayer in short order, or we may tend to give up on it. Focusing on necessities, worries, or daily activities does not aid our growth in the Spirit or our desire to love and become one with the Lord— as necessary as these things may be. We Protestants can lose a lot of potential spiritually by limiting our prayer life to the mundane.

We can, however, pray in the Spirit and carry on our dialogue with God "beyond the narrow limits of clearly intelligible language."[46] Praying in the Spirit can open a window of spiritual depth in which nothing shall ever be the same. I would like to provide a vignette to illustrate the supernatural utility of *glossolalia*.

During World War II the Aircraft Carriers, USS LEXINGTON and YORKTOWN, were under attack by enemy aircraft in the Battle of the Coral Sea off the coast of

Australia. The date was May 8, 1942. I was a twenty-one-year-old seaman aboard the YORKTOWN.

The YORKTOWN had taken one bomb hit mid-ship. At the same time the LEXINGTON could not repel enemy air attacks. As a result, LEXINGTON took two torpedo hits in the sides of the ship and two bomb hits from the air—all in four minutes. The ship was afire from stem to stern. Broken aviation fuel lines fed the flames with volatile aviation gasoline, and this generated numerous explosions. At the last minute the commanding officer of the gallant ship barked his final orders to his crew—"Abandon Ship!"

Henry ("Hank") Johnson, a photographer, had been badly burned in the explosions and was being treated for shock and burn in the ship's hospital. But when they were ordered to abandon the ship, the hospital turned its patients into the open sea.

In a daze and in excruciating pain, trying to escape the swirling vortex of water that a sinking ship draws with it, his strength now nearly spent, Johnson decided to give up and go down with the ship. He could take the pain and exhaustion no longer.

At that precise moment, however, heaven's communication system had been called into action. Far away in Providence, Rhode Island, the sailor had a Spirit-filled sister who had felt a strong compulsion to intercessory prayer five or six hours before the battle commenced. She did not know why she had this terrible burden. She knew nothing of her brother's predicament, but she obeyed the leading of the Spirit and went to prayer, praying in tongues, *glossolalia*, manifesting the Spirit—whatever you choose to call it.

She prayed in the Spirit for several hours. Then the moment arrived when she felt a great sense of release from the burden of prayer. She felt that spiritual victory had been won. But she still did not know the 'why' of her burden, or the result of her intense prayers.

However, at the precise moment she felt a release in her spirit, her brother, bobbing up and down in the water off the sinking aircraft carrier ten thousand miles away, heard the voice of the Spirit call out to him, "Try once again." At that moment a small boat approached and threw him a line and pulled him away from the sinking aircraft carrier.

Though his sister did not know what to pray for, the Holy Spirit did, and made intercession through her for her brother. Again, we note the 'butterfly anointing' that Dutch Sheets speaks of. Thus praying in the Spirit not only enhances the prayer life, but it makes the power of God available beyond what we can ask or imagine (see Ephesians 3:20).

Do not for one moment be tempted to think that your decision as to whether to speak in tongues could not also be a life and death matter for someone. If you want God to do greater works in your and others' lives, you might try giving Him more to work with.

A fifth reason to pray in the Spirit is that it is the gateway to the dynamic manifestation of the gifts of the Spirit listed in I Corinthians 12:1-7. The Pentecostals and the Charismatics are the people who are interested in these gifts, and they manifest these gifts in their churches—particularly, tongues, interpretation of tongues, and prophecy. These gifts are given to enhance spiritual worship and to edify the Church body as well as to make converts. I would like to share another vignette, which helps to make my point even clearer.

Years ago a Jewish salesman was in San Diego on business for his New York firm. His father was a rabbi. Sunday approached, and as businesses were closed for the day, he had nothing to do. But he rose, dressed, and went for a walk down the street to make his plans for the day.

As he waited at the crosswalk, the Sunday school bus from the First Assembly of God church drove up and stopped to take some children on board. The salesman stepped onto the bus along with the children and was promptly delivered to the church. It was a whimsical thing to do, but he was in a rather lackadaisical mood, having no plans for the day. But the Spirit of God had plans for him.

The worship and praise service was spirited and lively that Sunday morning, with about five hundred people in attendance. Then an odd thing happened. A small, elderly lady rose out of her pew and began to speak aloud and distinctly—in Hebrew!

The merchant's ears perked up. He understood every word she was saying. "But what was the Jewess doing addressing the congregation?" he wondered. At the conclusion of the service he approached the pastor and asked to speak with the little 'Jewish lady' who had addressed the body in Hebrew that morning.

He was introduced to the sister and spoke to her in Hebrew. Not having understood one word he said, she did not respond. Then he realized that she was not a Jewess at all. Now he was confused and desired to know the meaning of all that had transpired.

The pastor explained that what he had witnessed was the gifts of the Holy Spirit in operation. God was speaking to His people in that manner. It was a message of salvation. The result was that the Jew knelt and accepted Jesus as his Messiah-Savior.

Three days later he received the baptism with the Holy Spirit and spoke in tongues. He told us that he was planning to return to New York to tell his rabbi-father about the Messiah, the Lord Jesus Christ. In the operation of the manifestation gifts of the Spirit, God did in a few moments what our education and logic, perhaps, could never have done in winning that son of Abraham to God.

A sixth reason for praying in tongues is for the edification of the believer. The word, 'edify,' means to strengthen one spiritually, or to build up one's faith and spiritual life—to improve oneself. In a word, it is therapeutic.

In regard to the therapeutic affect of speaking in tongues, Marilyn Black Phemister, a Catholic writer and bookstore owner, told the marvelous story of her complete healing and deliverance from the state of depression after she received the baptism with the Spirit.[47]

She had moved from one city to another and located next door to a Pentecostal lady who soon learned of her depressed spiritual and mental state. The Pentecostal lady told Marilyn that she needed the baptism with the Holy Spirit and offered to pray with her.

She explained to her Catholic neighbor that as they prayed, the Spirit might put strange sounding syllables in her mind. If this were to happen, she should yield to the Spirit's prodding and speak them out. The two bowed their heads in prayer.

After a few moments of prayer, the Spirit began to move upon Marilyn. In her mind she was beginning to hear unfamiliar and strange sounding syllables as the lady said she might. She said she felt foolish to speak out syllables that she did not comprehend, but she began to utter them. Softly, she began to pray in tongues. The words came slowly at first, and then fluently. Marilyn said,

> I continued practicing [the words of the prayer language] and by the second day my depression began to disappear. My personality began to change. The third day with my prayer language I found myself sitting alone, clapping and singing and shouting, 'Praise the Lord,' at the top of my lungs.
>
> She discussed her newfound joy and conclusion that with God's presence a reality in her life, depression had lost its hold and she could walk life's road with power and joy. She had

experienced what tongues-speaking Christians throughout the ages have found to be true: the purpose and benefits of the baptism with the Spirit are numerous and bring manifold blessings and health to the believer.

Jesus' baptism in the Spirit gives us power for Christian service, for the development of the personality, for the enhancement of the prayer life, for strength to endure the stresses of daily life and for edification.

Last but not least, believers should desire to speak with tongues because the Lord desires it for us. Acts 1:4 and 5 read:

> On one occasion, while he was eating with them, he gave them this command: 'Do not leave Jerusalem, but wait for the gift my Father promised, which you have heard me speak about. For John baptized with water, but in a few days you will be baptized with the Holy Spirit.'

We are in no position to question what our Commander-in-Chief desires for us. Why refute His orders? Why argue with Him? Why not embrace all that He has to offer us? Remember, someone's life may be at stake. And for sure, your own and others' well-being is at stake.

You often hear the question, "Does not tongues-speaking cause division among God's people?" Let us admit that in some instances it does, just as religion in men can cause wars. But remember, they are people that cause divisions and wars—not God's Spirit. The enemy can and does wreak havoc using any tool that He can. Let us not blame God for man's actions.

When believers on each side exemplify a Christ-like attitude toward one another, divisions need not occur. Speaking in tongues does not of itself divide the Church. The attitudes and actions of His people, however, may divide the Body.

Some adamant Pentecostals feel that each worship service must be dominated by the manifestation of spiritual gifts such as tongues and interpretation of tongues. Hence they show little respect for those who do not join in. This can cause an attitudinal difficulty. Prejudice and spiritual arrogance can cause division. In this case it would not be those who do *not* speak in tongues that cause the difficulty, but those who *do*. Of course, arrogance among those who do not speak with tongues can also lead to division in the Body.

A balance is to be maintained if all are to enjoy the worship service together. Each side must give and take a little. This give and take attitude has been coming about since the great Charismatic Movement of the 1960's. We appear to be working better together, the classical Pentecostals and the Neo-Pentecostals or Charismatics.

The Religious News Service has reported that "The contrast in worship that once made the two camps distinct—lively and enthusiastic in the case of Pentecostals, and more staid and rationalistic on the part of Fundamentalists—is breaking down"[48] Fundamentalists have shed some of their dogmatism on theological issues, while the Pentecostals have moved toward the center. The latter are showing increased interest in theology, not just in religious experience. We seem to be moving closer together.

Paul set in order the regulations for the use of the gifts in the worship services in I Corinthians, Chapter 14:26-29:

> When you come together, *everyone* (italics mine) has a hymn, or a word of instruction, a revelation, a tongue or an interpretation...If anyone speaks in a tongue, two-or at the most three- should speak, one at a time, and someone must interpret. If there is no interpreter, the speaker should keep quiet in the church and speak to himself and God.

But Paul said to the church at Thessalonica who had

apparently lost appreciation for the gifts: "Do not put out the Spirit's fire; do not treat prophecies with contempt. Test everything. Hold on to the good" (I Thessalonians 5:19-21).

The Apostle Paul said in I Corinthians 14:5 (literally), "I desire that you all speak with tongues." Then in verse 39: "Therefore, my brothers, be eager to prophesy, and do not forbid speaking in tongues."

Rather than becoming a divisive doctrine, speaking in tongues can be a unifying experience for spiritually minded believers. It tends to keep people alive and vibrant in their testimonies and prayer lives. And remember—someone's life may be at stake. So then, let us eagerly "Be filled with the Spirit" (Ephesians 5:18).

Chapter Six

THE PEBBLE IN THE POND

When Can the Believer Receive?

A letter arrived from Japan that read:

> Dear Dr. Linzey:
> I heard Colonel Myrl Allinder speak at the Full Gospel Business Men's Fellowship Chapter in Tokyo. He said that you had laid hands on him when he received the baptism with the Holy Spirit. My wife and I plan to attend the World Convention of the Full Gospel Business Men's Fellowship, which convenes in Anaheim, California, in July. Would you do me the honor of meeting with me and pray that I may receive the baptism with the Holy Spirit?
> S/S Masatoshi Yoshimura
> Advisor to the Board
> Sanyo Chemical Industries
> Kyoto, Japan

Colonel Allinder, who had received the Spirit at our meeting in the Pentagon, now commanded the Marine Fighter/Attack Squadron 251 in Japan. Mr. Yoshimura had heard Allinder speak in Tokyo. As a result of Allinder's compelling testimony, he wanted the same experience. I responded that I would meet Yoshimura in Anaheim for prayer.

Verna and I drove from our home in Escondido to Anaheim. We located the motel where Yoshimura and his wife were staying and gently rapped on the door. As it slowly opened, we met the lovely, elderly and distinguished Japanese couple. They greeted us warmly. Mrs. Yoshimura was a Charismatic Catholic Christian lady who spoke no English. Being an international businessman, Mr. Yoshimura spoke English.

After a few words getting acquainted, I spoke to Mr. Yoshimura about praying in the Spirit. After a while he asked us to lay hands on him and pray. He calmly and quietly began to speak with tongues "as the Spirit gave utterance." The presence of the Lord was real in that motel room. It had instantaneously been transformed into a little chapel.

After some time in prayer, Verna and I gathered our belongings and prepared to leave for home. But Mr. Yoshimura insisted that he and his wife take us to brunch. We agreed and together made our way across the parking lot to a small restaurant to enjoy a pleasant time of fellowship as we ate brunch together.

Upon leaving the café we were walking to our car and expressing gratitude for prayer and our meal together. All of a sudden the four of us halted abruptly in the middle of the parking lot, spontaneously raised our hands toward heaven, and praised and worshipped God aloud, speaking in tongues. It was as natural as could be. We all agreed that if the unregenerate can cuss, smoke, chew and spit in the parking lot—or worse—then we could worship and praise God and talk in tongues in the same lot.

The delicate Japanese lady concluded our prayer in the parking lot that day. And this time when she prayed, she spoke in perfect English (tongues for her), "O, Hallelujah! Thank you, Jesus! Praise the Lord."

We had come full circle. The Spirit had begun a work with Chaplain Bob Warren in Albuquerque, which led to our meeting at the Pentagon where Colonel Myrl Allinder received his baptism, and this led to Allinder's sharing with Mr. Yoshimura in Japan, which led to his infilling in Anaheim.

What a chain reaction! Like the proverbial pebble in the lake, you don't know where or how the Holy Spirit will bless your labors as you speak and move for Him..." Jerusalem, Judaea, Samaria, and unto the uttermost parts of the earth" (Acts 1:8). You might help save a life as the sister did for her brother during the war, or you might help to set a captive free, like the paralytic woman in the wheelchair we referred to earlier. Freeing people in the Spirit is also its own reward.

It is beautiful to see how the Spirit of God keeps moving, for "The wind blows where it will" (John 3:3). As these ministries continue over the years, only eternity will reveal the scope and extent of the Spirit's work.

When Does The Believer Receive The Holy Spirit?

There are diverse opinions among Pentecostals as to the time of the reception of the Spirit. As I mentioned earlier, some believe He comes in a 'second blessing,' or in an experience or process of 'sanctification' subsequent to salvation. I have been clear all along that a person receives the Spirit at the time he or she accepts Jesus Christ as Lord and Savior. Evangelicals, if not all of orthodox Christendom, accept this stance.

When a person receives Jesus as Lord and Savior, the

Holy Spirit, the Third Person of the blessed Trinity, enters his heart, making him a child of God. Jesus said, "If any man loves me, he will obey my teaching. My Father will love him, and we will come to him, and make our home with him" (John 14:23). Peter said in his Pentecostal sermon,
> Repent and be baptized, every one of you, in the name of Jesus Christ so that your sins may be forgiven. And you will receive the gift of the Holy Spirit. The promise is for you and your children and for all who are far off—for all whom the Lord our God will call (Acts 2:38, 39).

Paul said in Romans 8:9:
> You, however, are controlled not by the sinful nature but by the Spirit, if the Spirit of God lives in you. And if anyone does not have the Spirit of Christ, he does not belong to Christ.

It follows then, according to these texts, that all Christians receive the Spirit when they accept Jesus Christ. This must be the starting point for agreement by all Christians no matter which tradition they hail from.

Some zealous Pentecostals attempting to lead fellow Christians into the Pentecostal experience inadvertently misuse the text. They quote John 14:17: "...he lives *with* you, and will be *in* you." In this passage He was predicting a future event. It had not happened yet. Up to that time the Spirit had not been given, since Jesus had not yet been glorified (see John 7:39). The Holy Spirit could not come until Christ was risen and glorified. At the advent of the Spirit at Pentecost, that is when the Spirit was poured out on Christ's disciples, this Scripture was fulfilled. John 14:17 can no longer be used to prove that believers do not have the Holy Spirit within them. That period of time lasted only forty days while they were waiting for the Promise of the Father. Ever since Pentecost, all Christians receive the Spirit at the moment of salvation. Jesus said in John 16:7,

> But I tell you the truth: It is for your good that I am going away. Unless I go away, the Counselor will not come to you; but if I go, I will send him to you.

Look at it this way. The Spirit dwelt with the disciples within the Person of Jesus Christ when He was on earth. "For in Christ all the fullness of the deity lives in bodily form" (Colossians 2:9). "For God was pleased to have all his fullness dwell in him..." (Colossians 1:19).

Then Christ was crucified, died, and was buried. He arose on the third day as He said He would, and forty days later ascended into heaven. On that first Pentecost after His death and resurrection, He returned in the Person and power of the Spirit, and entered the hearts of His disciples. Since the ascension He enters into the hearts of believers at the time of their acceptance of Him. This permits a closer relationship than Him merely being 'with' them, as wonderful as that surely was.

Professor Alec Vidler, the English theologian, reminds us that the activity of the Spirit was limited to the Person of the incarnate Christ when He was in Palestine.

> It was the death of Jesus which meant the settling free of the Holy Spirit for all. The Holy Spirit could be given in His fullness only when Jesus had been glorified by His crucifixion, resurrection, and exaltation to the throne of God. Christ ascended that He might 'fill all things,' and now the Holy Spirit could be poured out upon all men, and His recreating work within mankind could be extended universally.[49]

At Pentecost the sound from heaven and the tongues as of fire signaled that Jesus had reached heaven and was glorified. The Father had accepted the Son's sacrifice and had given Him the Holy Spirit (Acts 2:33) to give to His disciples.

Ever since Pentecost, believers receive the Spirit at the

time of salvation. Therefore, to experience the Spirit's manifestation (tongues), one must not expect an absentee Spirit to descend from heaven and enter into him (when He is already there) and thus force him to speak in tongues. Rather, the believer can in prayer and praise, expect the Spirit Who is within him to enable him to pray in tongues as He gives the utterance. Think of it this way, the Spirit within is always pulsating, awaiting a moment of manifestation. It is up to us to yield to the Spirit and allow the manifestation to occur.

There has been a longstanding misconception suffered by many old-time Pentecostals regarding the text in Luke 24:49 (KJV) concerning the word "tarry." It reads: "And, behold, I send the promise of my Father upon you: but tarry ye in the city of Jerusalem, until ye be endued with power from on high."

The word "tarry," which means, "wait," is understood by some to be Jesus' command for believers of all time in all places to wait for a second blessing for empowerment before beginning ministry. This is a tragic misunderstanding and has led many believers into a life of stagnation, fear and despair.

Prior to Pentecost believers did not have the indwelling Christ; hence, they had no inherent power. But since Pentecost Christ has come to dwell within believers; thus, we now have power for service. The baptism with the Spirit enhances that power and is a gateway to the gifts of the Spirit.

Jesus' disciples were not 'born again' in the New Testament sense until Pentecost when the Spirit came. They had to wait, for "up to that time the Spirit had not been given" (John 7:39). Were they saved? Of course they were, but not in the New Testament sense that future believers would come to be, those who did not know Jesus in the flesh. They were a part of the redeemed community in the Old Testament sense, just as were Abraham, Isaac, and Jacob and the Old Testament saints who looked forward to Calvary.[50] After that first Pentecost there is no record of converts waiting for the coming of the Spirit when they accepted Christ.[51]

The disciples were in Jerusalem with Jesus after the resurrection and prior to the ascension. During that time Jesus gave them commandments concerning the reception of the Spirit. Among other things He told them to wait for the promise of the Father: "Stay in the city until you have been clothed with power from on high" (Luke 24:49). Pardon my vernacular, but I like to put it this way: God was saying, "Don't leave town without it." So they waited for His promise. The "clothing of power" was and is the reception of the Spirit.

A question arises at this point: if all believers have received the Spirit, why are not all exhibiting power in serving Christ, in manifesting the spiritual gifts, speaking in tongues, or in witnessing for Christ?

The answer may be that many do not know that they have power potential or the capability of spiritual manifestation. Some are dispensationalists who relegate miracles and spiritual power to the first century Church. Some have been taught that they cannot have New Testament authority in their lives. In some cases believers do not pursue these blessings and are content to remain as they are: in a lukewarm or non-committal spiritual state. One of my daughters calls it "half-baked."

Some may live in a comfort zone and do not wish to be disturbed by the Spirit or the Church. The world-system has tranquilized some into spiritual numbness and inactivity. They do not wish to get involved. Some may fear emotionalism, but this fear obviously does not extend to ball games and worldly entertainment. Then some Christians just do not seem to care anymore. They have 'dropped out.' Jesus warns us against the attitude of complacency and smugness (see I John 2:15, 16; I Corinthians 13; and Revelation 2:5). The point is, it is incumbent upon us to help believers become aware of their potential in Christ and to urge them on to spiritual fullness and commitment.

Some have interpreted the forty days waiting at Pentecost to be a period of prayer in which everyone searches his heart and confesses all known sin so as to be 'worthy' of the Spirit. Because of this many have put themselves through hours and hours of horrendous introspection only to amass unbelievable guilt. Guilt then accrues in a cyclical fashion—guilt upon guilt. This robs one of joy and potential. We will never be 'worthy' of God's Spirit and His gifts. Let us accept His free grace and be thankful.

Introspection means to look inward to examine one's own heart or mind. It seems so right, and it is right in its proper time and place. There is a time for soul searching as the Spirit leads. There are times when a person should look inward, to self-reflect and to see if his relationships with God, others and self are in good standing. It wouldn't hurt some of us to do more of it.

However, others look inward in the endeavor to find good in themselves—an intrinsic good, worthiness, or righteousness that would enable them to rationalize their deserving of the fullness of the Holy Spirit—only to find that there is no essential goodness within. In the attempt to find good, they discern that they are indeed sinners after all, and that no merit on their part can bring the blessings of God (see I John 1:8-10).

The prophet said, "The heart is deceitful above all things and beyond cure: who can understand it?" (Jeremiah 17:9). In searching for good within and not finding it, guilt results. This can lead to a state of desperation and a sense of total worthlessness. This search can be spiritually and psychologically debilitating, leading to despair and unending self-condemnation.

Quite often these people are basically not happy. Their thirst for righteousness has backfired and they have inadvertently become self-centered instead. Ironically they do not find joy in serving the Lord. The cure for this disposition is to become Christ-centered instead of self-centered. Forget oneself and love the Lord is the antidote, "for He is worthy to be praised."

We need to see Pentecost for what it is—a festival. The people of God were eating and drinking, shouting the glory and thanking God for the harvest. They were a joyous people. The occasion for the festival was not particularly for confession of sin and atonement. That was reserved for Yom Kippur, the Day of Atonement. Rather, it was an occasion for rejoicing and a time for thanksgiving. In like manner, Pentecostal and Charismatic believers generally are a happy and joyous crowd—as well they should be. They have much to be thankful and happy about. Tony Campolo said it right when he titled his book, "The Kingdom of God is a Party."[52]

Pentecost was one of the three great Feasts in Israel: Passover, Pentecost, and Tabernacles. It was celebrated fifty days after Passover (*pente* means fifty). This Feast was an agrarian festival—the harvest of first fruits in which the community gave thanks to YAHWEH for His goodness in supplying them with food for another year.[53]

The command was, "Rejoice before the Lord your God" (Deuteronomy 16:11). It was celebrated with much joy and it was an occasion for covenant renewal. Later it began to be known as a celebration for the giving of the Law of Moses.

Israelite Feasts were times of rejoicing and excitement with ceremonial dancing, songs and many processions to the Temple.[54] All mature males in Israel were required to attend the Feasts if they possibly could.

Note the fulfillment of these Feasts: (1) Christ was crucified at the Feast of Passover, "The lamb slain from the foundation of the world" (Revelation 13:8); (2) The Holy Spirit descended at the Feast of Pentecost, revealing that Christ had been glorified (John 7:39) and His sacrifice for sin had been accepted; and (3) The Feast of Tabernacles, yet to be fulfilled, we believe will be the "Ingathering" of the Church, which will occur when Christ returns to take the Church out of the world—what is often termed the *rapture* (I Thessalonians 4:13-17).

Pentecost was a festive day. They had received His Spirit. The English Biblical expositor and minister, G. Campbell Morgan, said,

> But here upon the day of Pentecost, that which happened was not merely the renewal of the life of these men; it was the imparting to them of a new germ of life, a new principle of life, something they had never had before, that Abraham never had; there was given to them the life of Christ, the Incarnate One.[55]

The Messianic Age of which Joel had spoken, (Joel 2:28; Acts 2:17-21), was ushered in on Pentecost. This was a historic day indeed.

This is not to say that believers are not to be cognizant of sin or unconcerned about our sinful deeds and tendencies. We understand that sin and evil cannot stand before a holy God. But, we also know and believe that "The blood of Jesus, [God's] Son, purifies us from every sin" (I John 1:7); and that "There is now no condemnation for those who are in Christ Jesus" (Romans 8:1). Hence, we come to Him, on His merits alone. He has forgiven us; therefore we can rejoice and be happy.

We are righteous, but our righteousness is an imputed righteousness—a righteousness that is by faith" (Romans 1:17). Remember, "All our righteous acts are like filthy rags" (Isaiah 64:6). God the Father sees us through the Cross of Jesus and it is that which makes all the difference. We have worth in that He considers us worthy. We are holy in that, by His grace, we have been chosen for salvation. We are sanctified—set apart (I Corinthians 6:11). We are redeemed through His blood alone (Ephesians 1:7). Therefore, we have reason to rejoice.

As we have seen, misunderstanding of Scripture has caused great difficulty for some people concerning the reception of the Spirit. We must be clear and we must get it straight. There is no reason or excuse to be hazy or foggy theologically on such an important point.

Acts 5:32 is another example of misinterpreting Scripture, which leads to unrealistic expectations. "We are witnesses of these things, and so is the Holy Spirit, whom God has given to those who obey him." This Scripture is often quoted suggesting that a person must be obedient to God in every detail of his or her personal life; otherwise God will not give His Spirit. This is an untenable command.

In context this verse neither suggests nor implies perfect and complete obedience for Christians to receive the Spirit. Peter was preaching to the Jews, the Sanhedrin, on this occasion, which had authorized their persecution. The disciples had performed many signs and wonders in Jesus' Name (Acts 5:12), and were being held in custody for these acts. Peter preached to them while making his defense. He said in Acts 5:30-32:

> The God of our fathers raised Jesus from the dead—whom you had killed by hanging him on a tree. God exalted him to his own right hand as Prince and Savior that he might give repentance and forgiveness of sins to Israel. We are witnesses of these things, and so is the Holy Spirit, whom God has given to those who obey Him.

Peter was calling to the Jews for a decision to follow Christ [i.e., to obey Him]. If they would accept Him, they, too, would receive the Spirit, as had the disciples.

Never has any believer obeyed Christ completely and absolutely in all ways. If there were such a possibility that someone had fully obeyed in all aspects, a case might then be made for a 'works' basis for salvation. A reading of James won't let us get away with that, however. Rather, God saves sinners and fills believers, and then helps us to live more holy lives. It is liberating to realize this because this realization frees us to draw nearer to God. Men and women, and boys and girls must come to God just as they are.

> Just as I am, without one plea
> But that thy blood was shed for me,
> And that thou bidd'st me come to thee,
> Oh Lamb of God, I come! I come!

Another great hymn rings out:

> Nothing in my hand I bring,
> Simply to thy cross I cling;
> Naked, come to thee for dress,
> Helpless, look to thee for grace.
> Foul, I to the fountain fly;
> Wash me, Savior, or I die.

One concomitant question is yet to be raised and answered, and that is this: since the Holy Spirit is given at the time of conversion, when is the baptism with the Spirit received? We have touched on it previously, but let us explore it further.

Andrew Murray, the great South African pastor and theologian, clearly distinguishes between 'rebirth' and the 'manifestation of the Spirit's presence.' He considers them to be two parts of the same promise. He said, "Where faith claims it, the second half of the promise is fulfilled as surely as the first."[56]

He then asks rhetorically, "How are these two parts of the divine promise fulfilled—simultaneously or successively?" He answers by saying, "From God's side the twofold gift is simultaneous. It appears that we men have made it a succession of steps."[57] He realized that the doctrines of conversion and the baptism with the Holy Spirit had been bifurcated by churchmen. Actually, God's viewpoint and plan in the New

Testament was that it was to be one work of grace. He adds, "When the standard of spiritual life in a church is sickly and low...we must not wonder that, even where God gives His Spirit, He will be known and experienced only as the Spirit of regeneration."[58]

The point is that the saving act of God is a complete act. This means that God planned that men and women should get saved, sanctified and baptized with the Spirit and live Godly lives for Jesus.

It is a package deal. He had not planned that a person could get saved without sanctification and the reception of the Spirit. Nor does it mean that one could get saved and sanctified but not receive the Spirit. The plan of salvation is deficient if any one of these three items is excluded or lacking. It should all be one salvific event.

Theologians today have dissected the plan to study the parts but left them to stand alone to be studied as individual doctrines, independent of one another. It is helpful to discuss salvation, sanctification and speaking in tongues, one item at a time in order to better understand them. In actuality, however, they were meant to occur simultaneously. Experientially the parts stand together in unity as a whole.

To reiterate, some Pentecostal groups make salvation a matter of stages: first a person gets saved; second, he gets sanctified; and third, he receives the baptism with the Spirit. Three works of grace. Some groups skip the sanctification step, attaching it to salvation and end up with two steps of grace: salvation and the baptism with the Spirit.

However, God did it all at Calvary when Christ died for our sins. He completed the Plan with the resurrection of Christ from the grave and the giving of the Spirit at Pentecost to believers. It is one Grand Plan.

The manifestation of the Spirit (tongues) was, and is, a sign of the completion of the Plan. The giving of the Spirit at Pentecost signaled that Christ had reached heaven and had appeared before the Father. The sacrifice of His blood for our sins had been accepted. The Father then gave the Son the Holy Spirit to give to His disciples and believers (Acts 2:33). And following this we all grow in grace and knowledge of our Lord and Savior Jesus Christ (II Peter 3:18).

God's Plan is that men should get saved and speak in tongues—saved, and on the same occasion manifest the Spirit. This is the New Testament pattern, or paradigm. The Pentecostal power is not meant to be subsequent to the saving act.

In order to maintain a logical discussion of doctrines and experiences, it becomes necessary to consider prior and subsequent acts. But God certainly did not intend for us to make speaking in tongues a subsequent act of ten, twenty or thirty years after receiving Christ. This is needless and tragic. It is meant to be a package experience—receive and manifest. And the power is for everyone (Acts 2:38, 39).

Harold Horton, the noted Pentecostal Scholar and Harvard graduate said,

> There is absolutely nothing in the Scripture one degree like what we call a 'waiting meeting' today, where, say, a dozen come to seek the Spirit and all go away disappointed, only to come again...week after week, month after month, year after year. [59]

We have found in our seminars that once a Christian understands his own involvement in the tongues experience, and feels at liberty to engage in it, he manifests the gift readily. This should be a normal spiritual experience to be desired by all Christians. It is a blessing that all believers should desire and experience.

Chapter Seven

CAN GOD MAKE A MISTAKE?

Who May Receive?

I was ministering for the Sunday morning and evening services in a small church near the Long Beach Naval Shipyards. There were about twenty-five people in attendance, a small but vocal group who enjoyed their faith and expressed it in outward praise. In the morning service I presented a brief overview of the doctrine of the Holy Spirit. In the evening service I invited those who desired prayer for the manifestation of the Spirit to join me near the altar. A sailor and an elderly man rose and stepped forward. The sailor was a Roman Catholic young man who had not yet personally accepted Christ—though I did not yet know it.

In my invitation I had stated, "Tonight I will be pleased to lay hands on anyone who desires to receive the baptism with the Holy Spirit. I don't care who you are, how you are living, or what you are doing with your life at the present, as long as you love Jesus."

I found out later that the reason the sailor was in the service was that he was dating a young woman in the church and the girl's mother had ordered her daughter to go to church that evening. Wanting to be with the girl, the sailor consented to go with her.

When he arose to come forward for prayer, a lady sitting on the back pew of the little church became alarmed at my ignorance of the fact that the sailor was not 'saved.' Fearing that I would lay hands on an unsaved Catholic was more than she could bear. With no time to waste, she cupped her hands and in a hoarse whisper that could be heard all over the little church, she announced, "He's not even saved!"

Well, I got the word all right. In fact, the whole church got the word, that is, everyone but the sailor. Having never been in a Pentecostal church, he did not know what she was talking about. Nor did he know that she was talking about him. So he continued to come forward.

We were in uniform that night—I, a Navy Commander, and the sailor, in bell-bottom trousers. He stood before me at rigid attention as if he were terrified to be standing before an officer. I asked him, "Son would you receive the Holy Spirit when I lay hands on you?"

"Yes, Sir!" He replied.

I leaned over the pulpit and placed my hands on the sailor's head and said, "Receive the Holy Spirit."

When I laid my hands on him, he closed his eyes as if in excruciating pain and lowered his head. After a few moments, he lifted his head, opened his eyes wide, raised his arms to heaven and cried out to God, "Save me! Save me!" and began speaking in tongues as he stood before the congregation.

God heard his prayer. He saved the young man and baptized him with the Holy Spirit—instantaneously! He manifested the gift by speaking in tongues. This is how it should be.

God accepted him as he was, a sinner desiring mercy, then saved him and blessed him with His Holy Spirit. This is the way God works, for He is a gracious God. Following this experience, the sailor would be discipled and taught the things of the Bible. He would be encouraged to "Grow in grace and in the knowledge of our Lord and Savior, Jesus Christ" (II Peter 3:18).

Who May Receive?

Another time I concluded a seminar and called those to come forward who desired prayer and laying on of hands for the manifestation of the Spirit. Ten or twelve people responded, and all of them easily manifested the Spirit. In addition, all the members of the congregation rejoiced around the altar that night—all but one!

I had instructed believers to come to God for the Spirit's manifestation regardless of how they perceived their state of sanctification, or degree of holiness. After observing the service and the spiritual blessings poured upon all classes of people, a visiting Pentecostal evangelist approached me. "May I speak with you?" she asked.

"Please do," I responded.

She appeared to be upset and a little angry. She shook her finger at me and asked rather emphatically, "Did I hear you correctly to say that God would fill anyone with the Holy Spirit without due regard to personal holiness?"

"Yes, Ma'am. That's correct," I replied. I could see her problem.

"Do you mean to tell me that if a man has been out last night drinking and carousing around with women, that if he came to the altar tonight, God would fill him with the Spirit?" She was aghast.

"I certainly do." That's what I preach."

"I can't believe that," she said. "Doesn't he have to repent?"

"Surely he does, but doesn't his coming to the altar for prayer indicate repentance and a desire for God?"

"I can't accept that," she huffed, and offered a few critical remarks. She had evidently fallen into a form of legalism that demanded that a person take steps to God in a prescribed manner in order to receive His blessing. From her frame of reference she could not understand how God could possibly have blessed the person she had described.

"What do you want the person to do?" I asked. "What more could one do to manifest the Holy Spirit?" She simply shook her head in disbelief. Rather than enjoy the move of the Spirit with the group and praise God for His acceptance and His goodness toward His people, the lady resented God's sovereignty in blessing others whom she felt unworthy (or at least my teaching that God would accept and bless sinners while cleaning them up) and stomped out of the auditorium. It reminded me of the elder brother in the story of the Prodigal Son who could not rejoice to see his wayward brother warmly accepted by the father when he returned home (see Luke 15:11-32).

On another occasion after hearing my sermon, a person said, "You seem to make the Holy Spirit so common."

"Perhaps," I said. Apparently He does become common to dwell in people like you and me, doesn't He?" Jesus was God Almighty; He became incarnate so man could approach a holy God. It is the same with the Spirit. Jesus said, "Whoever comes to me I will never drive away" (John 6:37). *This means anybody.*

Please do not misunderstand me. This is not to denigrate our church's position on holiness, per se, but it appears that some people do not understand the meaning of the term. We have neither time nor space here for a full treatment of the doctrine of holiness, but basically holiness means to be singled out, to be selected, to be chosen, to be set apart. God has chosen us for Himself and set us apart [from the world system] for His glory. He has sealed us with the Holy Spirit (see Ephesians 1:13); He has put His stamp upon us. We are His. Positionally, we *are* holy. We are holy because He made us holy, not because we became holy through acts of righteousness (works). Basically this is the meaning of the term. Peter said in I Peter 2:9:

But you are a chosen people, a royal priesthood, a holy nation, a people belonging to God, that you may declare the praises of Him who called you out of darkness into his marvelous light. This is holiness. It is a finished work from God's viewpoint.

However, as to our conduct, we are to "purify ourselves from everything that contaminates body and spirit, perfecting holiness out of reverence for God" (II Corinthians 7:1). And, "without holiness no one will see the Lord" (Hebrews 12:14). It is our part to work out holiness in our walk and conduct, and it is done as we "Grow in the grace and knowledge of our Lord and Savior Jesus Christ" (II Peter 3:18). We clean up our act, so to speak, as we are conformed to His likeness. The Holy Spirit will help us do this.

What are the conditions that one must meet to receive the Spirit? Are there any? Just this—that a person loves Jesus Christ and seeks to serve Him and do His will. Holiness cannot signify perfection. Perfectionism and sinlessness surely are not the prerequisites to attain the blessing. If such were the case, none of us could receive it. Contrary to some people's opinions, perfection of character is not going to be attainable in this life, though it is our aim, our goal. The greatest saints of the Church have considered themselves the greatest of sinners. Paul said, "Christ Jesus came into the world to save sinners—of whom I am the worst" (I Timothy 1:15).

The fact is, the closer a person gets to God, the greater he feels his sinfulness. Isaiah felt it when he said, "Woe to me...I am ruined! For I am a man of unclean lips...my eyes have seen the king, the Lord Almighty" (Isaiah 6). After all is said and done, we are sinners saved by grace. We can thank God for His grace and mercy and blessing. Peter said in Acts 2:21: "Everyone who calls on the name of the Lord will be saved." Jesus said in John 7:37-39:

> If a man is thirsty, let him come to me and drink. Whoever believes in me, as the Scripture has said, streams of living water will flow from within him. By this he meant the Spirit, whom those who believed in him were later to receive. Up to that time the Spirit had not been given, since Jesus had not yet been glorified. He said in Luke 11:13,
>
>> If you then, though you are evil, know how to give good gifts to your children, how much more will your father in heaven give the Holy Spirit to those who ask Him?

The conditions are that one asks and drinks—desires and receives! Regardless of a person's education, wealth, race, and color, all are invited to partake of the blessings of the Spirit. As the Sunday school song says,

> Red and yellow, black and white;
> All are precious in His sight.
> Jesus loves the little children
> Of the world.

One evening as we were praying for the sick, I approached a young man and inquired as to his particular need for prayer. "I want to become a Christian," he earnestly replied.

I led him I prayer in which he confessed himself to be a sinner and asked God's forgiveness. He asked the Lord Jesus to come into his heart and make him a child of God. As we stood around the altar praying with him, I said, "Now raise your hands and begin to thank God for saving you," and he readily did so. Then I laid my hands on his head and said, "Receive the Holy Spirit."

The rest of us were praying in the Spirit and I encouraged him to do likewise. He began to pray in tongues fluently. In a few moments this young man had been saved and spoke in tongues. This is the expected New Testament pattern of which I speak.

Dr. Charles Farah, former Academic Dean of Oral Roberts University, recounts how the early Church functioned in methodology and practice in this regard. He said,

> It was the experience of the early Church that [the laying on of hands] was the medium through which the Holy Spirit was conferred on people who had been baptized...A man believed, was baptized, and as he came up out of the water, had hands laid on him for the reception of the Spirit. It is the sign by which a man is constituted a sharer in the apostolicity of the apostles of Christ in carrying out the Lord's commandment to bear witness throughout the world.[60]

Who may receive the baptism with the Spirit? Anyone who desires it. There are no prior conditions attached. This was vividly portrayed some time ago and made real to me in another amazing encounter.

The service was over and the prayers around the altars had hushed. I retreated to the rear of the large auditorium where a lady greeted me. She was an exuberant woman who told me of her experience.

"Chaplain," she said. "You were in this church three years ago."

"That's right, I was." I replied.

"You made the same opening statement tonight that you had made three years ago when you were here...you said that you would lay hands on all who desired to receive the baptism with the Holy Spirit regardless of their spiritual condition, as long as they loved Jesus."

"That sounds like something I would say," I answered.

"You did!" she exclaimed loudly "I was here. You laid hands on me and I received the baptism with the Holy Spirit." Then she related the rest of the story.

"When you were here three years ago, I had been saved

for only two weeks. You laid hands on me and I received the Spirit. At that time I still swore; I smoked; I danced; I gambled; and I drank. You laid hands on me and I received the baptism with the Holy Spirit."

"Well, how are you doing now?" I asked.

Her face lit up and she radiated joy when she exclaimed, "I'm all cleaned up!" We clapped our hands and hugged and praised God for His marvelous grace!

The point is that *God took her where he found her spiritually.* He saved her, and though she needed a lot of cleansing (sanctification), he blessed her with His Spirit. He knew her heartfelt desire was to love and serve Him, so He trusted her with His Spirit to enable her to begin living a holy life. In time, by his indwelling Spirit, He helped her clean up her act.

This is the way God seems to do it. He takes us where we are spiritually and makes us what He wants us to be. Truly, any Christian who loves and desires to serve Jesus Christ may receive this blessing.

Chapter Eight

SPIRITUAL SECRETS TO GOD

How to Manifest the Spirit

The scene was the Pasadena Cafeteria and the occasion was the monthly dinner meeting of the Full Gospel Businessmen's Fellowship. I was to be the speaker to about 125 men and women who would gather for dinner and fellowship with a program including music and personal testimonies.

I had been asked to speak on the baptism with the Spirit. When I extended the invitation to those who desired to manifest the Spirit, about 18-20 people responded including a meticulously attired professional woman. (Businesswomen were included in the fellowship meetings.) She was the first person to stand in line to be prayed for that evening. I proceeded to give her verbal instructions as to how to cooperate with the Spirit in the manifestation of tongues. Those standing around were also listening.

"When a child is born into the family," I explained, "he has no language, no vocabulary; he cannot speak. But as he lives in the family, he hears words from the family members and he often mimics them. Parents encourage this pattern of speech development because they know the child is learning how to talk. So the child practices his language and eventually speaks articulately. He does not concern himself with the physical mechanics of speech; he just opens his mouth and blabbers until he gets it right.

"When I lay hands on you," I continued, "I shall begin to speak in tongues, and others shall be praying in tongues around you. If it will help you, take a word from me, or from one of the others around you to get started. It will free you to speak and God will give you your own prayer language."

When I finished my instructions I asked the lady if she understood this.

"Yes, I do understand," she replied. "You see, I am a language teacher; this makes perfect sense." Needless to say, she spoke in tongues easily as did the others.

I admit that there has been a degree of criticism in some quarters from those who think that I 'tell' people what to say to manifest the Spirit. But this is not accurate, nor is it my intent at all. It *is* my aim, however, to provide and establish a climate of faith and encouragement that will enable those seeking to get started speaking in tongues.

Initially using a word that a person has heard from someone else praying in tongues may be useful as a catalyst. The praying group provides the opportunity and the atmosphere for movement into the spiritual experience. Once a person begins to speak in tongues, God gives him his own prayer language.

We need not—nor can we know—all about the development, mechanics or psychology of speech. We can, however, manifest the Spirit by speaking in tongues as "The Spirit gives utterance," and as we speak out in faith.

Dr. W. Lee Martin was professor of speech at Indiana University. Concerning the mechanics of speech he said, "It takes 65 movements of the tongue muscles to say the words, 'Philadelphia, Pennsylvania.' But we do not stop to think about these movements of the tongue muscles, or we would not speak at all. We just talk.

He continues, "When a baby begins to speak, he does not begin with an articulate language or he would never speak. He must learn his language and he learns by cooing apparent gibberish, and we encourage him in this for we know that articulate speech will eventuate." He implied that it is the same with speaking in tongues.[61] We can learn from Prof. Martin. Small wonder, then, that Jesus said we must become as children to enter into the Kingdom of God.

How May One Manifest The Holy Spirit?

When it comes to manifesting the Holy Spirit, we would do well to study the various steps that lead to that end. Like rungs of a ladder, let's ascend them one at a time.

First, believe that it is God's will for you to manifest the Spirit. The gift is for ordinary believers, as well as exceptional or talented persons. Jesus said,

If you, then, though you are evil, know how to give good gifts to your children, how much more will your Father in heaven give the Holy Spirit to those who ask him? (Luke 11:13).

Peter said in Acts 2:39: "The promise is for you and your children, and for all who are far off." It is for all who believe. Paul said further, "I would like everyone of you to speak in tongues" (I Corinthians 1:5a). It is God's will for you to manifest the Spirit and speak in tongues.

Second, decide that you want to manifest the Spirit. Simply decide to do so. Many Christians are passive or blasé in stepping out and taking hold of the promises of God. Paul told us that we should pray in the Spirit in all circumstances (see Ephesians 6:18). So, we have to involve our will in the matter, which leads to acceptance and manifestation. ***It is your decision.***

Third, be willing to pay the price of complete surrender.

When we seek for the manifestation of the Spirit, the recipient must offer himself in total surrender. He must take his hand off his own life, for he now belongs to another, Jesus Christ.

He is going to serve the Lord whole-heartedly from this point onward, and now he is free to manifest the Spirit. The heart's cry is, "Well up within my heart, O Lord, and overflow." Jesus said,
> Whoever drinks the water I give him will never
> thirst. Indeed, the water I give him will become
> in him a spring of water welling up into life
> (John 4:14).

So, say to yourself, "I welcome you, Holy Spirit; come into my life in your fullness. I receive you now."

Believe that He does come in as you give yourself to Him, and begin to worship, uttering the strange-sounding syllables that may come to your mind, and you will be expressing the gift in its manifestation as you pray and praise in the Spirit.

The final step is to go ahead and manifest the Spirit—speak in tongues. The manifestation of the Spirit is proof-positive that one has received the Spirit. Peter made this clear concerning the Gentiles' acceptance by the Jewish Church in Jerusalem when he said:
> They heard them speaking on tongues...The
> Holy Spirit came on them, as he had come on us
> at the beginning...God gave them the same gift
> as he gave us...(Acts 10:46; 11:15; and 11:17).

In Acts 2:4, we note that they were filled with the Spirit, "And began to speak in other tongues as the Spirit enabled them." One reading says, "They began to speak with tongues as the Spirit gave them this ability to speak out."[62]

First, they had to receive; second, they had to speak out; and then the miracle occurred—the connection between the human and Divine was made. Man spoke

"Spiritual secrets to God."[63]

Upon receiving the Spirit, a person must begin to speak in tongues by faith. The Spirit then takes over and gives the miracle of divine utterance. This is consistent with the scriptural principles of faith. Throughout biblical history man has cooperated with God's plan by activating his faith. For example, in Exodus 14:16 Moses had to stretch forth his rod *before* God parted the Red Sea. This was an act of faith in obedience to a command.

In I Kings 17 the widow had to make the prophet a cake *first* before God gave her the miracle of the multiplied meal and oil. In each of these instances each person had to ***do*** something by faith ***before*** God responded. So we encourage men and women to ascend the ladder; take the steps of faith and speak in their heavenly language. This is scriptural.

Someone may respond, "I want to receive it by faith *alone*." Or, as one man told me when I prayed with him, "I want **God to do it**." Now, while that may sound 'holy,' this wish is born of fear, not faith. The simple fact is that this man did not wish to initiate action. How convenient to have God do it all. We must remember that faith requires action on our part. Faith *is* action. Faith is something we ***do***. We 'faith' it. The Lord does not force this gift (or any other gift) upon us. We must desire it and willingly enter in to manifest it.

The question arises, "Just how does a person begin to speak in tongues?" In reply, I would answer that he begins the same way he begins to speak in his native language, or any acquired language—as a baby learns to speak.

He makes a sound or speaks a syllable. A succession of sounds or syllables makes up words, hence, sentences and language. The Holy Spirit translates these sounds into divine communication. Even though the person himself verbalizes, it is the Spirit who performs the miracle of language beyond the person's mental capability. One may make a verbal sound to get started and believe that God will honor his faith and help him continue.

Self-consciousness is a hindrance to many believers. Society is made up of self-centered people for a good part. We have taught each other to be so self-conscious of how we act, think and especially feel, that for too much of our lives we are stymied or paralyzed into inaction. This is sometimes reflected in the way we pray.

At times when we pray with folk to manifest the Spirit, they shut their eyes tightly as if this will help to 'get into the Spirit' mode somehow. That is, they think they can bring down the blessing if they concentrate on it hard enough. God is 'out there' and we are 'down here.' We are separate and apart, not together. We are waiting for the Spirit to come in and to bring with Him the manifestation. We think that there is nothing for us to do, somehow, but wait.

This mode of thinking only causes people to become doubly aware of themselves—which actually takes their minds off the Lord. This waiting in intense self-awareness actually leads to inactivity, and paralysis—non-participation—rather than cooperation with the Holy Spirit.

The solution to our overly self-consciousness is for the person to realize that God is here in the now, even in his heart. We are united and God and I are together in this. Then the seeker can realize that he/she can verbalize the Sprit's manifestation volitionally, for He is present to validate it. The individual does not have to wait any longer.

When I voice out the sounds (which make up my prayer language), I can rest assured that the utterances are true and correct. Paul said, "Undoubtedly there are all sorts of languages in the world, yet none of these is without meaning" (I Corinthians 14:10). This is an important concept to grasp. *There will be no mistakes.* The solution is that one must get one's mind off himself and focused on Jesus.

One speech teacher asserted that articulate speech is the manifestation of the human spirit; it is a means of expressing one's own human spirit. Only humans have this capacity for such expression, for only they have Spirit. (Note that animals do not have spirit as humans do; hence, they have no articulate speech or self-reflection.)

So much more could be said for the human voice manifesting the presence of the Holy Spirit. We must by faith open ourselves to Him, release the Spirit within, and enjoy His presence in His fullness.

When one first begins to speak in tongues, it is natural for some negative thoughts or doubts to come to mind and hinder the expression. The first such thought usually is that the utterance cannot be 'real.' It seems too easy or contrived, or, it sounds strange or weird.

But let me assure you that this is the Promise of the Father. Pay no attention to these negative thoughts; keep on speaking in tongues because this is the open door you have been waiting for. Accept it readily and cooperate with God's plan and method of empowerment.

The second 'one-liner' the tempter raises is, "That's just *you* speaking." And my retort to this trickery is, "Well, *of course* it is *you* speaking." We take full responsibility for the faculty of speech while the Lord takes the responsibility for the language we speak. It is a faith venture—a cooperative action. You use *your* voice and God gives you *meaning*. At times some people are not even aware that they have manifested the Spirit because they have wrong expectations.

Don Basham, the eminent pastor and writer of the Disciples of Christ church, tells the story of a minister who had tarried long for the manifestation of the Spirit. One night in a small church, ministry was offered for those seeking the manifestation of the Holy Spirit. The earnest pastor made his way to the front of the church as he usually did. Upon reaching the altar, he flung himself down on the floor and began to pray. As usual, no one went to assist him because it never did any good. All of his friends had wearied themselves praying for him.

After a few minutes everyone was amazed to hear him begin to pray aloud in tongues in a beautiful, clear language. Then to their surprise the minister pushed himself up from the floor and said, "I don't want you people to get the wrong impression. I still don't have the baptism. I'm not speaking in tongues; I'm just making funny noises. I got tired of waiting on God to do it, so I just opened my mouth and babbled sounds. But, it is not the Holy Spirit. It is me!" (Sic).

Then it was the minister's turn to be surprised. Three young Chinese college students had been watching the proceedings from the front pew. One of them answered the minister, "Brother, you've bee praising God in perfect Chinese for the last three minutes and we understood every word you said."[64] Why challenge God Himself so that your expectations for manifesting the Spirit exceed His? Is it pride or fear at work here?

When others have seen the ease in which seekers manifest the Spirit in our seminars, some have commented, "But the way you do it seems so mechanical." What they mean is that it does not impress them as *spiritual* enough.

I understand what they are saying. And I apologize if the way I express it seems mechanical or 'unspiritual.' However, "we walk by faith, not by sight" (II Corinthians 5:7). We must not depend on our feelings or emotions to determine our spirituality—ever. When feelings are present we should be grateful for them. But to base decisions and judgments solely on feelings is great fallacy. When one learns to live by faith, many things in the Christian's life may seem to become mechanical in practice. But this is true in all walks of life. We do not make the same decisions every day. Many decisions are made and habits are thereby established.

However, we do not encourage excessive emotionalism either. Because of this, some have said, "Doesn't your method [laying on hands with prayer] give only a *minimal* experience?" I would disagree and say, "Not at all." If I could be a little facetious for a moment, I would add that if a person has not manifested the Spirit prior to meeting us in ministry, it would seem that *any* experience he might receive emotionally would be more than he had previously.

By the way, we do not discourage emotionalism either. Some people by nature are more emotional than others. Whatever state of mind people have carries over into their religious lives as well. Some shout easily, some cry and weep, some dance for joy when moved upon by the Spirit, some are slain in the Spirit or fall upon the floor under emotional impact. We have seen this and can appreciate it. But, let us not expect that all should react alike.

In reality there is no 'minimal' experience at all; but there are various and different degrees of emotional responses to the Spirit. Our preconceived ideas due to lack of knowledge often hinder us and keep us from the Spirit's manifestation.

Some people presume to evaluate the validity of the tongues experience themselves. That is, they try to determine or decide whether or not the tongue is a 'real language' that they are speaking. This is quite audacious and an impossibility in any case. Unless you can speak all ten thousand languages in the world, you are not qualified to make this assessment.

Sometime ago we prayed for a self-conscious young lady who desired the manifestation of the Spirit. She was discouraged and a little fearful. When I encouraged her to involve herself in prayer and speak out, she said, "I don't want it to be *me*!" I assured her that it would indeed be she when she spoke. She did not wish to follow me in prayer in the Spirit for she was afraid that she would be mimicking me in the prayer language. But I laid hands on her and prayed anyway.

She did not speak in tongues at that moment, but I told her, "You have the baptism with the Spirit. Now go home and practice your prayer language in the privacy of your home where you will not feel inhibited or embarrassed in front of all these people. Call me in the morning and tell me how it went." This was Sunday night.

The next morning, she phoned me at the pastor's home. She was excited as she told me her story. "I followed your advice," she said, "I went to bed and prayed, then dropped off to sleep. About 1:00 o'clock this morning I began to pray in tongues. I thought that since salvation is easy, the baptism with the Spirit should be easy to manifest. So I 'entered in' and received an incredible experience with the Spirit." When she understood her part in the process and readily cooperated with the Holy Spirit, she had her heart's desire—and the fullness of joy ensued.

Let me summarize what I have been saying. The manifestation of the Holy Spirit comes by a decision of the will. Paul said in I Corinthians 14:32: "The spirits of prophets are subject to the control of prophets." This means that the prophet can prophesy or stop from prophesying at will, for he is in control of his own spirit at all times, as are we all. This principle holds for all the verbal or oral gifts and manifestations. Paul calls self-control the fruit of the Spirit. God does not intend to take over our will. He wants us to voluntarily commit our will to Him. This is in keeping with the principle of self-control.

We can speak or cease to speak when we choose. This was dramatically demonstrated to me one day when I was stationed on the East coast. I met a Pentecostal Coast Guardsman in Newport, Rhode Island, at the Christian Servicemen's Center. He was a ship's cook serving in the Coast Guard's Square Rigger, the EAGLE. The ship had come to Newport from New York to monitor the yacht races held off the coast of Newport.

He was a young married man who had a wife and baby in New York. Due to the family separation, he was lonely, depressed and homesick. I sensed his need for Christian fellowship so I took him home with me to meet my family. My wife, Verna, prepared dinner. After dinner he asked, "May we talk about the Holy Spirit?"

"Surely," I replied. "What in particular is on your mind?"

"If I could pray in tongues, I would feel so much better," he said. "I think I wouldn't feel so depressed."

"Do you have the baptism with the Spirit?"

"Yes, I do," he responded.

"Then you can pray in tongues any time you wish."

"Oh, no, I can't," he rejoined.

"Why not?"

"I can only pray in tongues when the power gets turned on," he said.

"Well, how do you turn the power on?" I asked.

"That's what I don't know."

"I got an idea. I'll show you how to turn the power on," I told him. The Lord then led me into a spontaneous and most peculiar fashion to minister to this young man.

"I am going to lay my hands on you and then I shall count to three. When I shout, 'Go!' throw your hands up and open your mouth and pray in tongues."

"I can't do it," he muttered.

"Will you try?" I prodded. He said that he would.

I counted, "1-2-3-GO!" On hearing the word, "Go," he raised his hands and promptly began to pray aloud in the Spirit—in tongues. After a few moments of this praying, I stopped him. He looked at me in amazement and said, "I didn't know I could do that!"

This serviceman was surprised to learn that he had a part in the action with the Spirit. I then told him to practice his prayer language on a daily basis to become fluent in it. Practicing prayer produces fluency in prayer.

This was in the fall of the year. At Christmas I received a card from him which read in part, "Dear Chaplain: Merry

Christmas. Since I met you and learned that I can speak in tongues any time I wish, I do. Now the Lord has given me five or six different languages that I pray in." The sailor had learned to release the Spirit within, and now the Lord has blessed him with "different [various] kinds of tongues" (I Corinthians 12:10).

On another occasion after a wonderful Sunday morning service, sixteen men and women manifested the Holy Spirit for the first time. One was a young married lady whom we had met previously when the pastor and I had gone to see her husband in the hospital. God had been dealing with both of them about making an earnest commitment to Christ. They both had prayed and surrendered their lives anew to Him and spoke in tongues.

At about 5:00 o'clock in the afternoon the doorbell rang at the pastor's home. We opened the door to find the lady waiting outside. She was upset, nervous and doubted that she had experienced the manifestation of the Spirit. Furthermore, she doubted her salvation. She asked, "Will you pray with me and let me pray the sinner's prayer?"

"Of course," I said, "But first, let's talk about your doubts. You should not argue with them. It's like arguing with the devil. The more you argue with them, the worse they become. You can't win. Accept your doubts and trust God for victory."

She nodded in agreement. "Rather, you should begin to worship Jesus while the storms of doubt and testing rage. This way you can overcome your doubts and fears."

"Let's pray," I said. As Verna and I took her by the hand, I led her to pray the sinner's prayer, as she desired. She asked God to save her in Jesus' Name. Then I encouraged her to begin to worship and praise the Lord. We heartily worshipped together for some time.

Then I laid hands on her and encouraged her to manifest the Spirit in speaking in tongues. She readily prayed aloud in the Spirit with us. After a few moments, the joy of the Lord, like a torrent, rushed over her, flooding her soul and spirit as she began to rejoice. She jumped up and down, shouting, "Now I know I have it! I know I have it!" She had gotten a real victory and was all smiles. Assurance was hers.

When worship replaces self-consciousness and doubting, God can begin to move and have His way in our lives—even in our emotions. Joy may replace worry and fretting; doubts and burdens become manageable. No wonder the writer said, "Rejoice in the Lord always. I will say it again, rejoice" (Philippians 4:4).

Dennis Bennett, the Charismatic Episcopalian rector, was the principal speaker for the first trans-denominational conference on the Holy Spirit convened by the Assemblies of God in Springfield, Missouri. One evening he extended an invitation for 'seekers' to come forward for prayer and manifestation of the Spirit. Many responded with high expectations.

At the altar service his injunction to the assembled group was: "I am going to pray that God will baptize you with the Holy Spirit. You should know that this is an apostolic way of doing it. After I pray for you, I shall ask you to turn to the Lord with all your heart and praise Him, **but not in English**. Praise Him in tongues."

When he had concluded his prayer, upwards of one hundred and twenty people easily manifested the tongues experience in a short time. There was a wonderful time of rejoicing. I liked the methodology Bennett used. It is so simple and straightforward.

The blessing of the Holy Spirit is for all Christians. The Apostle Paul wrote to us in Ephesians 5:18-20:

> Do not get drunk on wine, which leads to debauchery. Instead, be filled with the Spirit. Speak to one another with psalms, hymns and spiritual songs. Sing and make music in your

heart to the Lord, always giving thanks to God the Father for everything, in the name of our Lord Jesus Christ.

How shall we manifest the Holy Spirit? Oral Roberts has advised, "Get with those who are praying in tongues, and open your mouth and make a start, and God will give you your own prayer language." Same methodology, same results.

Let us summarize the four steps that will lead one to manifest the Holy Spirit.
1. **Believe it is *God's will* for you to manifest the Spirit.**
2. **Decide that *you want* to manifest the Spirit.**
3. **Be willing to *pay the price* of a complete surrender to Jesus Christ.**
4. *Go ahead and manifest the Spirit*—**speak in tongues.**

As one ascends the ladder to God's fullness, he can readily manifest the Holy Spirit. God will then equip him with the power to influence others to come to Christ and experience God in His power and fullness.

Chapter Nine

THE ALTAR CALL

Is the News Good?

People who express a desire to manifest the Spirit need some understanding as to how God works with His people. He desires to fill them. A scriptural presentation and a promise that God will indeed meet their needs when they come to Him have proven effective in our seminars. Seekers respond promptly when we give the invitation.

I think that it is important to bring our people to a place of desire and expectancy for things of God. There must be a sequence of events and instruction to bring faith to action. Billy Graham has repeatedly demonstrated in his crusades that to move people toward God, they must be prepared spiritually and psychologically for the event.

In some meetings our task is to bring people from a state of apathy to that of renewed spiritual interest and desire—all in one session. This is not always easy, but it can be done with proper planning and prayer.

In the opening remarks in our seminars we inform the people that about 50 percent of the folk in our Pentecostal churches do not pray in the Spirit. Perhaps you are one of those who have not yet experienced praying in the Spirit.

I then take a survey in the congregation as to how many currently speak with tongues. I ask for a show of hands. I ask that those who do not speak with tongues to raise their hands. They freely comply. I thank them for their honesty and willingness to respond and then go into the message. Those who are reluctant to raise hands the first time are the ones who often raise hands the second time and respond to the invitation of prayer.

In pursuing this method I have obtained somewhat of a commitment from the seekers prior to preaching. They are in attendance for a definite purpose. The groundwork has been laid. At the invitation, responses then come more easily with group participation and seekers readily move forward. The following is how I approach my message to the assembly. There is good news for them.

Is The News Good?

Yes, it is. There is also good news for you who wish to manifest the Holy Spirit speaking in tongues. One piece of good news is that Jesus wants to bless you with the power of the Holy Spirit. The second piece of good news is that to manifest the Spirit, God does not require perfectionism on your part—no particular degree of holiness, as you may perceive it. You can receive the blessing right now in your present spiritual condition. Spiritual growth indeed will ensue. The requirement is that you love Jesus Christ and wish to serve Him faithfully.

I then go on to explain how an imperfect view of holiness, that of sinless perfection, has caused some people to quit seeking the blessing. They think they are not 'good enough' to approach the Lord, and that He will not accept them in their less-than-perfect-spiritual condition. They know themselves to be less than perfect. They know that they have spiritual problems to work out. Some have adopted the idea that God will not accept them until they 'clean up their act.'

However, they have found that they cannot clean up their act without the Spirit's help. This posits a 'catch-22' dilemma, a paradoxical one with no solution. Since they cannot, or have not resolved their personal problems, they are inhibited to approach God for His Spirit, which could actually help them resolve these very issues. Hence for some, the search for growth in God ceases, or at least is greatly diminished.

No one is completely and perfectly 'holy' in act or deed. "As it is written: 'there is none righteous, no, not one'" (Romans 3:10). This is true for saint and sinner alike. We must always come to God as we are. And we are always deficient. "While we were still sinners, Christ died for us" (Romans 5:8).

I then continue my instructions: "We do not require that you 'tarry,' or wait as is found in Luke 24:49 (KJV), a text which the Church has often misunderstood. Many pulpits have preached that believers must attend a 'waiting' meeting and spend a specific amount of time in prayer until God *empowers* them with the Spirit. Many of you have followed this plan only to be disappointed so many times that you no longer seek His blessing.

David A. Womack relates the experience of the Reverend Donald Gee of England many years ago. Reverend Gee relayed that an Irish brother asked him if he were saved, to which he replied that he was. He then asked if Gee had been baptized in water. Again, Gee affirmed that he had been. Then the question as to whether he had been baptized in the Holy Spirit. Rev. Gee replied that he had not. Then he was asked, "Why not?" Reverend Gee said, "I explained my aversion to the apparently weary tarrying times."

The brother then explained that Gee need not tarry and read to him from the Bible Luke 11:13: "If ye then, being evil, know how to give good gifts unto your children; how much more shall your heavenly Father give the Holy Spirit to them that ask him" (KJV). And Mark 11:24: "Therefore I say unto you, what things soever ye desire, when ye pray, believe that ye receive them, and ye shall have them" (KJV).

The Irish brother asked Pastor Gee if he believed the promises. Gee replied that he did indeed. Rev. Gee said, "As I declared my faith, it seemed as if God dropped into my heart from heaven an absolute assurance that these promises were now being fulfilled in me.

> "I had no immediate manifestation, but went home supremely happy, having received the baptism in the Holy Spirit by faith. This went on for about two weeks. Then one night, when praying by my bedside before retiring and finding no English adequate to express the overflowing fullness of my soul—I found myself beginning to utter words in a new tongue."[65]

Donald Gee's experience may seem strange to traditional Pentecostals who cling to the idea that tarrying is a must in order to experience the outpouring of the Spirit. Perhaps, more strangely, that Gee claimed to have the baptism with the Holy Spirit without the initial physical evidence of speaking with tongues, which came later for him.

The same may be said for Pastor Lewi Pethrus, who pastored the Pentecostal church in Stockholm, Sweden. He pastored the church for years without the tongues experience. Then one night he laid hands on a man in his church and prayed for the brother to receive the Spirit. At that moment he, that is Pethrus himself, manifested the Spirit and spoke in tongues for the first time.

Tarrying has produced much unbelief among God's people who have prayed so earnestly without success. They need only realize that the Holy Spirit was given once for all on the Day of Pentecost. The Spirit has been in the Church

The Altar Call

and the world ever since. One needs only believe and act on this to find his heart's desire, the blessing of Pentecost.

One should not demand an emotional response to prove that he has received the Spirit, though he may have an emotional experience. Often, well-meaning people attempt to measure their spirituality by their feelings. This is neither fair nor proper. Emotions, per se, may be misleading, or a false gauge of one's spiritual state.

As previously pointed out, we do not belittle emotions. We have seen some individuals express a great display of emotional outburst on occasion as they respond to the Spirit. People react differently and these reactions are intensely personal.

One lady asked, "But won't it give you a spiritual lift?" Yes, it will, but in God's good time. God knows when you need a spiritual lift, and He will provide for it. The desire for emotions may lead one to wrong expectations: an emotional 'high,' or immediate gratification of feelings, or some type of euphoria. While it is true that this sometimes does happen, it is my experience that it may not, and generally does not, occur.

Heather, a seventeen year-old girl brought her Baptist grandmother to me for prayer so that she might manifest the baptism with the Spirit. The elderly lady was apprehensive about it all, and made it very clear.

Furthermore, she had a heart condition and was afraid that emotionalism might physically damage her. I explained that emotions were not necessary to manifest the Spirit and that she need not be afraid.

I took her by the hands and told her that I was going to pray quietly in the Spirit—tongues—and that she should simply join me in praying in the Spirit. I asked if she would try. She agreed. I then prayed softly and asked Jesus to fill her with the Holy Spirit.

Grandmother began to pray in tongues in a whisper, in

an unemotional manner. Then she spoke audibly. Finally, she was speaking fluently and clearly in tongues "as the Spirit gave [her] utterance" (Acts 2:4). She testified the following night in the church service. She was radiantly filled and showed it.[66]

I was the speaker for the West coast convention for the Samoan Assemblies of God in Carson, California. Over 1,000 people including their pastors met in the Carnegie Junior High School. Reverent Pita Leasau, the General Superintendent for the national body, asked that I instruct his people in the doctrine of the Hoy Spirit. He realized that many of them needed to manifest their baptism.

The music was good, the worship spirited, and all joined in. The glory of God came down in the auditorium and a great anointing rested on the congregation. I gave the invitation and many responded. In my instructions I said, "When I pray for you to manifest the Spirit, open your mouth and make a start. God will give you your own prayer language." I followed this by saying, "When I pray for you, hold your heads high and worship God, not in English or Samoan, but in tongues. Others gathered with us for prayer.

An exuberant outburst of praise and worship commenced when 20 to 30 Samoan men and women began to worship the Lord in tongues. One Islander, tears flowing down his cheeks, all-aglow with the Spirit, grasped me and said, "I've been seeking the Spirit for years. Now I have Him!"

The late Dr. James McKeever, the internationally known consulting economist and author from Medford, Oregon, was a speaker for the Full Gospel Businessmen's California/Nevada Regional Convention, which convened in Modesto, California in February 1991. He gave a presentation on the Holy Spirit, and on his appeal, 41 men and women responded to receive the Spirit. I led the group to an assembly room for further instruction and prayer. Others gathered to assist in ministry.

The Altar Call

I informed them that they 'had' the Sprit; because they were believers, and that when we laid hands on them they were to join the prayer group and pray in tongues. God was moving and His presence was felt deeply. After briefing them, I had them raise their hands and worship in English to begin vocalizing praise to God. Then I prayed and asked God to fill them.

In a moment's time all forty-one men and women manifested the Spirit. An emotional time of praise and worship followed their reception. Dr. McKeever wrote me later, saying, "forty-one in one night: that's exciting!"

How Do I Receive This Baptism?

When one-on-one, I describe to the believer how the experience of speaking with tongues might come about. In a pubic meeting we have learned that some who desire to manifest the Spirit may not be truly converted to Christ at the time. When we sense this, or especially when we feel that some may have been involved in the occult or the drug scene, we lead them in a prayer of deliverance.

Those with a questionable past must denounce false beliefs, demonic spirits and drugs, and invite Jesus Christ into their hearts. The Holy Spirit is good and kind to give us discernment in these particular cases.

Having prayed, we then lay hands on them, pray over them and encourage them to enter in and embrace the Spirit by faith and manifest the Spirit. The altar call for salvation is always appropriate, and in most cases, the filling of the Spirit ensues.

Upon preparation and presentation, where apathy has been turned into spiritual interest, where believers have a felt need and a desire to be filled with the Spirit, Jesus meets His people and baptizes them with the Holy Spirit. No particular forum is necessary, no particular setting, whether it be in church, at home, driving the car, or whatever; "They who call upon the name of the Lord shall be saved"—and filled!

Paul said, "Be filled with the Spirit. Speak to one another with psalms, hymns and spiritual songs. Sing and make music in your heart to the Lord, always giving thanks to God the Father for everything, in the name of our Lord Jesus Christ" (Ephesians 5:18-20). In so doing, the Church may be a powerful Church, a victorious Church, an effective Church, and a happy Church. Therefore the injunction, "Be filled with the Spirit."

Epilogue

IS ALL THIS NECESSARY?

Some time ago a seminary professor conducted a five-day seminar for ministers. The instructor lectured in the morning sessions and fielded questions in the afternoons after the lunch break. In the concluding session a young minister asked, "Doctor, is all this theology really necessary?"

The old professor gazed out the window for a few moments in contemplation. Then he turned to the preacher and remarked, "I think so. It is helpful and it is interesting."

He continued, "The Christian life is like a symphony. The movement opens with a simple one-line melody. Other instruments join the strings as the piece progresses, adding to and creating variations on the theme. Finally the rendition reaches a climax. All the instruments are in accord. The sound of music reverberates in the halls. They have enhanced the basic theme, the melody. When the orchestra nears the end of the performance, various instruments begin to diminish until only the simple melody, the main theme, is heard again. It has been interesting."

This is analogous to the Christian life. A person accepts Jesus as Lord and the symphony begins. He has been given a simple melody, "Jesus loves me, this I know." That's the theme. This is all one has to know to be saved.

His Christian life progresses and, as he matures in years and in the faith, he desires expansion, or variations on the theme. He studies the Bible, attends prayer meetings and preaching services to expand his knowledge. These instruments embellish the theme. They are helpful.

Finally, he passes his prime and comes to old age. As he nears the end of his life, he may not need all the theology any longer. The instruments begin to fade away and the movement tapers off. At the end he is back to where he began—with the simple melody, "Jesus loves me, this I know." That's the theme. That's all he needs to know, but the embellishment and power on the theme in his life has been helpful and fruitful. It has intrigued him and stimulated growth.

The understanding and experience of the manifestation of the Holy Spirit and His gifts add to the beauty and power of the Christian life. Countless believers around the world pray in their spiritual language. Their lives have been enriched and emblazoned with power because they have accepted the promised Holy Spirit that the Father in His Divine Plan and wisdom has made available to them. The Holy Spirit and His gifts embellish the theme, "Jesus loves, me, this I know." He is helpful and he has made the Christian life stimulating and fruitful.

PART TWO

Questions and Answers

Questions and Answers

In Part I we studied the doctrine of the Baptism in the Holy Spirit. We cited appropriate examples to validate the biblical claim that the baptism with the Spirit and its manifestations are for believers today just as they were in New Testament times. We showed that by the simple act of faith and obedience believers may avail themselves of these blessings. These are ready and waiting for the taking.

Questions may yet arise about the Spirit or spiritual gifts and their operations. You may feel that some issues have yet to be dealt with. In Part II we will endeavor to answer many of the questions that remain and hopefully clarify some points of misunderstanding.

We have found that people are generally asking the same kinds of questions wherever we travel. People want to know more about the Spirit and His gifts and they desire teaching.

What I present here are spontaneous questions asked from various members of audiences in our meetings after periods of instruction. They are not presented here in any particular sequence. They may be selected at random for study in Bible classes Sunday school classes, seminars, or midweek meetings, as the need arises. We hope that these are useful.

Some questions have been purposely left open-ended. This leaves space for further discussion in the group setting, and can lead to fruitful discussions in

Bible study. The questions are listed in the Table of Contents for easy reference.

QUESTION 1: The Catholics and the Neo-Pentecostals have experienced the manifestations of the Sprit for only a short time and they appear much happier about it than we Pentecostals who have enjoyed this experience for a long time. May it be that we have had the blessing for too long, have had it too easy, and/or do not appreciate it as we should?

ANSWER: Yes, it is possible that we have had the experience—not necessarily too long—but perhaps too easy. At times a person may be tempted to take his blessings for granted. They may become commonplace. However, there is also the maturation process to consider.

For example, you may have noticed that when a person is born again, the new Christian is excited and happy, generally energetic and enthusiastic about his new life in Jesus. He wants to tell everyone about it. He may even get emotional about it. This is well and good.

However, in time he grows up in the Lord and matures. While he hopefully will remain appreciative of his salvation and the filling with the Spirit, he may become more factual and seasoned about it and less visibly emotional due to the maturation process. Hopefully he will not ever lose his zeal for Christ, however.

Catholic Pentecostals and Neo-Pentecostals also go through this process. However, a deep joy should remain with the believer. Every believer should feel that it gets better as we go along. "Rejoice evermore, Pray without ceasing. In everything give thanks; for this is the will of God in Christ Jesus concerning you" (I Thessalonians 5:16-18).

QUESTION 2: Why do most prayer languages sound repetitious and why do some people's prayer languages sound alike? Should they not be more varied? Are we

Questions and Answers

repeating ourselves over and over?

ANSWER: Many Charismatic/Pentecostal believers' prayer languages may sound repetitious because they use or speak a limited number of words or sounds with which they feel comfortable. They might attempt to expand their spiritual vocabulary in tongues. This can be done. When praying in the Spirit one should consciously and knowingly cause himself to utter new and different words "as the Spirit enables" him (Acts 2:4).

God does not make us or insist that we maintain a particular language. Rather, we must be free and open to change, unafraid to speak out and express ourselves. It is our gift, our prayer language. We can speak freely and at will.

I should point out, however, that what the unlearned ear might perceive to be repetition may not be that at all. Languages often have various nuances and inflections that go undetected by the untrained ear. Perhaps we should not call any sounds of tongues (languages) 'repetitious.' Let each seek to expand his/her own prayer language in worship and praise.

QUESTION 3: If it is true that when a person speaks in tongues, it is his/her own spirit that speaks, and not the Holy Spirit speaking through him, (as we have so often heard), then how does my spirit know what to pray for?

ANSWER: The Apostle Paul said in Romans 8:26, "...we know not what we should pray for as we ought..." This can be true when praying with the conscious mind, as well. When we pray with our understanding (conscious mind) we may pray selfishly for our own desires, or for our own will in a given matter. Unthinkingly, we may be biased or dishonest. But, "if I pray in a tongue, my spirit prays" (I Corinthians 14:14).

Praying in the Spirit is praying from the deep subconscious, the true self, in all its honesty, desire, and will. This type of praying bypasses the natural intellect, which tends to influence our will and desires. The real person addresses the Father "in spirit and in truth" in this praying (John 4:24).

Because of this possibility, Paul commanded, "Pray in the Spirit on all occasions with all kinds of prayers and requests" (Ephesians 6:18). This is an imperative! One can only obey this command if he has experienced the baptism with the Holy Spirit and spoken in tongues.

Our Spirit is inspired by the Holy Spirit to pray for what, or for whom, we should pray, even though we may not know the situation or the people for whom we are praying. He puts it in our hearts to pray. "The Spirit intercedes for the saints in accordance with God's will" (Romans 8:26).

QUESTION 4: Can a person receive the baptism with the Holy Spirit without speaking in tongues? Please explain?

ANSWER: We shall not tell God how to baptize a person with the Holy Spirit. We know of people who have had hands laid on them with prayer for the reception of the Holy Spirit, who claimed the promise, and did not speak in tongues at the time. But later they did manifest the Spirit.

The Reverend Lewi Pethrus, founder of the Pentecostal Church in Sweden, was such a person, as was Donald Gee of England. Gee claimed the promise of Luke 11:13, "...how much more shall your heavenly Father give the Holy Spirit to them that ask him?" He spoke in tongues a couple of weeks later.

This does not seem to be the normal way to receive the baptism, however. In the Book of Acts believers spoke in tongues on every occasion when they received the gift. Please go back and reread Chapter Two of this book.

It was an observable and objective experience that proved to the believer and others that he had received the Spirit and that he was saved. Peter used this argument with the Jewish Church to prove that God had accepted the Gentiles (Acts 10). The appearance of *glossolalia* [tongues] was how they knew.

Today, many believers want to reduce the occasion to a subjective experience, which needs no validation. If a person wants to be certain he has a New Testament experience, he should insist on New Testament evidence (see Acts 2, 10, and 19). As an aside, if a person could speak in tongues, and will not, a good question is, "Why not?"

QUESTION 5: May a person receive the gift of devotional tongues when he has no intention of discontinuing the use of tobacco or other drugs?

ANSWER: Yes, this is a possibility. When most of us came to Christ for salvation, or the baptism with the Spirit, our intentions may not have been absolutely pure; We may not have known at the time all that Jesus would desire of us, or all that we would want to surrender to Him.

God accepts us as we are, flaws and all. Then He begins to mold us into His image. At the moment of salvation, we begin to "grow in grace, and in the knowledge of our Lord and Savior, Jesus Christ" (II Peter 3:18). We would expect that the believer would also desire to be conformed to Christ's image. But let us refrain from judgment if he/she does not. This is not our place.

God does not call for perfection of character or intention at the invitation to come. It takes the Holy Spirit to bring that to pass. Once one has become a Christian, however, his performance should begin to shape up as he desires to be like Christ.

The idea that a person must be perfect to come to Christ has kept some people from seeking the manifestation of the Spirit. It is like asking a person to clean himself up before he takes a bath. He may get the tub dirty and he knows it. But perfecting oneself before coming to God is not really possible. This fear and awareness of being 'too dirty' has kept some people from coming to church and seeking all that God has for them.

The Holy Spirit is a gift, as is salvation. It is not a reward for good works. We should be inviting people to come to Jesus as they are. The Church is a hospital, not a country club. He will mold them into His image in His good time.

QUESTION 6: Those who criticize the 'tongues-talkers' say that tongues is not needed today. They quote I Corinthians 13:8-10 as a proof text for their argument: "That which is perfect" is the canon of Scripture, and since all truth is contained therein, tongues shall cease. How do you answer them?

ANSWER: The text reads:

> Love never fails. But where there are prophecies, they will cease; where there are tongues, they will be stilled; where there is knowledge, it will pass away. For we know in part and we prophesy in part, but when perfection comes, the imperfect disappears.

Paul stresses in this text that love is of paramount importance in relation to the gifts, which will pass away. He named three of them: tongues, prophecy, and knowledge. These were the visible and highly sought after gifts, and the most abused. All gifts of the Spirit will cease when "that which is perfect" has come; namely, the Lord Jesus Christ. But the point is this: prophecies have not yet failed, nor has knowledge vanished away, for the Perfect has not yet come.

The gifts of the Spirit shall all cease, for they are transient. They are for the Church age alone. But the gifts shall all cease at the same time, when Christ comes for His Church. Since prophecy has not ceased, nor has knowledge vanished away, we must not insist that tongues have ceased—or wish they would!

When the Perfect comes, the gifts will no longer be needed. Jesus will be here in His perfection. We shall no longer "see through a glass darkly." We shall see Him as He is and "we shall know even as we are known" (I Corinthians 13:12). John said,

> Dear friends, now we are the children of God and what we will be has not yet been made known. But we know that when he appears, we shall be like him, for we shall see him as he is (I John 3:2).

The earth and the universe will have returned to its perfect state when the Lord Jesus, the Perfect One, comes. When the gifts of the Spirit will have ceased, having served the Church well, faith hope and love will continue into the Kingdom! But, all the spiritual gifts remain until that time.

"Even so, come, Lord Jesus!"

QUESTION 7: Please explain what you mean when you say, "Practice your prayer language."

ANSWER: A person should continue the practice of praying in the Spirit in his devotional life. Paul asserted in I Corinthians 14:15, "...I will pray with the spirit, and I will pray with the understanding also..."

Because of misunderstanding its value and purpose, some receive the initial tongues experience but fail to continue its use thereafter. They do not exercise a decision or volition to pursue it.

"I will pray with the Spirit..." (I Corinthians 14:15). Paul indicated that praying in the Spirit connotes determination, or an act of the will.

Some folk let their experience become dormant because of non-use. We urge people to keep praying in the Spirit on all occasions on a regular daily basis (Ephesians 6:18).

QUESTION 8: Is there such a thing as a counterfeit tongue? I have an acquaintance of the Mormon faith, which does not believe that Jesus, or the Holy Spirit, is God. However, she says that she speaks in tongues. How could these tongues be of God?

ANSWER: First of all, we do not know that she speaks with tongues, only that she says she does. While Mormons declare that they believe in speaking with tongues, this is not actually the case.

Mr. Bill McKeever, Director of the Mormon Research Ministry in El Cajon, California, and a former Mormon, has stated that Mormons are very vague on the subject of tongues. "They certainly have no Pentecostal experience," he said. "Their definition of the gift would be that they have the ability to learn a language!" Yet, Article Seven of the Articles of Faith, their official document, affirms that they speak with tongues. This poses a problem of semantics over a clever use of terms. When they say they believe in speaking in tongues, they are not saying what we think they are saying.

One does not have to be concerned with counterfeit tongues when seeking the baptism with the Spirit. The fear that tongues may be counterfeited has caused many Christians to be fearful of seeking God. They are afraid that they may get a 'wrong' experience.

The Bible says, "...how much more shall your heavenly Father give the Holy Spirit to them that ask Him": (Luke 11:13). We can trust Him to give us the Holy Spirit. We are safe in Him. There is no such thing as a 'counterfeit' tongue. There is no Biblical warning or statement about such a thing.

QUESTION 9: Please explain I Corinthians 14:13, "...the man who speaks in a tongue should pray that he may interpret what he says."

ANSWER: Paul is referring to the gift of tongues exhibited publicly in the assembly. He is not talking about devotional tongues practiced in one's private prayer life. In private prayer there is no need for interpretation, for no one but God is listening to the prayer. In the public meeting an interpretation must follow a message in tongues so as to edify and bless the church.

There are times when a congregation will be worshipping, and many will be singing or praising in the Spirit. This is well and good. It is a beautiful worship experience, and even though it occurs in the congregation, it is not meant to be a message that must be interpreted. It is the private use of tongues, experienced corporately. The public use of tongues occurs when one voice raises clearly above all others and addresses the congregation. This is what must be interpreted.

In the church at Corinth some spoke in tongues and failed to interpret the message in the language of the church for its own edification. No one profited by this procedure. We see this on occasion in some Charismatic and Pentecostal churches in America. It is not desirable.

QUESTION 10: In reference to I Corinthians 14:23, when our church worships, we all pray in unknown tongues out loud, all together. How do we know that we are not doing what the Scripture says not to do? The first time I went to a church that did this, it scared me and turned me away as this Scripture said that it would.

ANSWER: We know that we are acting properly, for the church has been taught to worship in a corporate manner. Ephesians 5:18-20 indicates corporate worship:

So if the whole church comes together and everyone speaks in tongues, and some who do not understand or some unbelievers come in will they not say that you are out of your mind? This verse deals with the abuse of the gift of tongues publicly in a meeting in the church, not to corporate worship.

No one should interrupt a public service with an unexpected outburst of tongues. The unbeliever may well think the one who does this is out of his mind. This leads to disorder in the meeting.

When prophecy, or tongues and interpretation are in operation, the guidelines are clear: "Two—or at the most by three—should speak, one at a time, and someone must interpret...Two or three prophets should speak..." (I Corinthians 14:27, 29).

On the Day of Pentecost the 120 spoke in tongues simultaneously. No one was offended. They were in awe, and perhaps, fearful. The result was that 3,000 were converted, baptized in water, baptized with the Holy Spirit, and added to the Church. These episodes have recurred in many places with the result that people get saved and filled with the Spirit.

A spirited Pentecostal service often inspires awe, consternation, or possibly discomfort to an unbeliever on his first visit to the church. It should! The church is not another social club based on its appeal to carnal delights.

> The man without the Spirit does not accept the things that come from the Spirit of God, for they are foolishness to him, and he cannot understand them, because they are spiritually discerned" (I Corinthians 2:14).

The inquirer states that it "scared him" and "turned him away." Paradoxically, he now finds himself a member of the church: saved and filled with the Spirit, doing the very thing in the corporate setting that he once feared. So, the spiritual service accomplished its purpose.

We need not feel ashamed of a good spiritual worship service, for God is at work in the service to inspire awe and reverence that can lead to faith and belief. One pastor remarked that when he became 'Pentecostal' his church began to grow. He conducts three Sunday morning services and two Sunday night meetings in addition to other services during the week.

We have been in meetings in which several thousand people worshipped in tongues and sang in the Spirit simultaneously. These were beautiful services in which many were saved, healed and filled with the Spirit.

QUESTION 11: If a person should accept the Lord over a television program by phone, but does not follow up by going to church and being baptized, will he still go to heaven?

ANSWER: It is not our business to sort out the wheat

from the chaff; that is God's business. However, what you have described is problematic. The question is not relative to water baptism, or even church attendance. Rather, it concerns itself with nurture, spiritual growth or maturation and discipline (see II Peter 3:18).

Today we know that 75 out of every 100 persons who come to Christ in America are stillborn, or live only a short time as a Christian. Research has revealed this staggering statistic: a whopping 75 percent! This is to say they come to the birth but die a premature death. They fall by the wayside or drop out.

Think of it! 75 percent of all who start out with Christ do not go on with Him! This may be due to poor planning and stewardship of money, people, plans and resources by those churches and groups who do not stress follow-up and discipleship.

Christians need the institutional Church for discipline, teaching, fellowship and service. We do not live in a vacuum. Please check out Matthew 28:19; II Timothy 3:15; and Hebrews 10:25.

Just as no one is an island, because we are all social creatures, so the Christian life is not lived in solitude, but rather in the context of the Christian fellowship and community. Church growth experts say that we should not count anyone as having been 'won to Christ' until he has joined the Fellowship. Elton Trueblood, the noted Quaker philosopher and scholar penned, "The fellowship is the Company of the Committed."[67]

However, I am not speaking of the sick, the infirm, the shut-ins, the imprisoned, or the terminally ill who cannot go to church. They are obviously excused. We must take the Church to them. Our Lord said that we should visit the sick and those who are in prison according to Matthew 25:35-40. Many of these would like to attend church. So we thank the Lord for providing Christian television for them.

While we do not wish to err on the side of legalism, we can suggest that the able-bodied and all those who can are encouraged to worship in the church of their choice on regular basis. Paul's injunction is:
> Let us not give up meeting together, as some are in the habit of doing, but let us encourage one another—and all the more as you see the Day approaching (Hebrews 10:25).

Are Christians who do not worship and fellowship with a congregation truly saved? That is a hot potato and we best leave that one to the Head of the Church Who knows all hearts. We are not privileged with this information. I might cautiously add that it doesn't look spiritually healthy, however.

QUESTION 12: Don't the Scriptures show that speaking with tongues must come from the Holy Spirit and not learned from 'practice?'

ANSWER: In my seminars I stress that those who receive the devotional gift of tongues should practice their prayer language on a regular daily basis.

The Bible says, "The Spirit enabled them to express themselves."[68] "They began to speak in tongues as the Spirit gave them utterance," or "the ability to speak out," or as "the Spirit enabled them." Paul said, "If I pray in a tongues, my spirit prays" (I Corinthians 14:14).

From these few expressions of Scripture it is readily apparent that the question is based on a misunderstanding of the texts, or the operation of the Holy Spirit within the human spirit.

We must affirm that the baptism with the Holy Spirit is a gift, which inspires and enables the person to speak in tongues. But the person has the power to control this ability. I Corinthians 14:26-28 teaches control and discipline in the act of speaking in tongues.
> When you come together, everyone has a hymn,

or a word of instruction, a revelation, a tongue or an interpretation. All of these must be done for the strengthening of the church. If anyone speaks in a tongue, two—or at the most three—should speak, one at a time, and someone must interpret. If there is no interpreter, the speaker should keep quiet in the church and speak to himself and God.

Two or three prophets should speak, and the others should weigh carefully what is said. And if a revelation comes to someone who is sitting down, the first speaker should stop. For you can all prophesy in turn so that everyone may be instructed and encouraged. The spirits of prophets [and tongues-talkers] are subject to the control of prophets [and tongues-talkers]. For God is not a God of disorder, but of peace.

In other words, when one speaks in tongues, it is not question of whether or not it is 'God' or the 'person' speaking. It is both God and the person who speaks or prays. God always invites cooperation from His people in the operation and manifestation of His gifts. One must practice the gifts the Spirit has given him if he is to become effective in the use of them. Spiritual operations require bilateral action on the part of the person and God.

QUESTION 13: How does one receive the ability to give a message in tongues after having received his prayer language? Or, how do you know you are to give a message in tongues?

ANSWER: This question concerns itself with the gift of tongues expressed publicly in the assembly, not with devotional tongues that all believers manifest when they are baptized with the Spirit or in private prayers.

The Scripture lists tongues as one of the manifestation gifts of the Spirit (I Corinthians 12:7-12). Verse 11 reads, "...all these are the work of one and the same Spirit, and he gives them to each man, just as he determines." The Holy

Spirit gives the gifts as He desires to whomsoever He desires. This is true of all the spiritual gifts.

On the other hand, we are told to "...desire spiritual gifts, but rather that ye may prophesy" (I Corinthians 14:1). Prophecy would likely be more helpful to a church full of believers than tongues—unless the gift of interpretation is also in operation for the edification of the body.

Note, when Paul says in I Corinthians 14, "...desire spiritual gifts, *especially* the gift of prophecy" (v. 2), and "...I would like everyone of you to speak in tongues, but I would *rather* have you prophesy" (v. 5), he is not saying prophecy is more desirable than tongues. He literally says, "I would like everyone of you to speak in tongues, *but more* (Gr. *mallon*) I would have you prophecy (italics mine). It is not a case for either/or—tongues or prophecy—but rather *both* are desirable.

Perhaps the second part of the question is more relevant. Those who speak in tongues publicly generally say they become aware of an inner desire to speak out. They sense an urgency to speak. They feel the Spirit urging them, or nudging them to speak. When one has experimented with the gifts over a period of time in the congregation, he soon learns to distinguish between the leading of the Spirit and his own mind.

The use of the gifts must be desired, then cultivated and practiced. The Lord allows us time and space to perfect the exercise of the gifts. One must first discover his gift (or gifts), then develop them with practice and prayer. To help you discover what your particular gifts may be, you might refer to Dr. Peter Wagner's book, "Your Spiritual Gifts."[69]

All God's people are a gifted people (I Corinthians 12:7). Each has a gift, gifts, or gift-mix. Let us discern our gift and function in that capacity, whatever it may be.

QUESTION 14: I Corinthians 14:15 states: "I will pray with my spirit, but I will also pray with my mind."

Please explain.

ANSWER: Paul had been attempting to correct the abuse of tongues in the Corinthian church. In such corrective measures he declared that each person is in control of his own spirit (v. 32). This principle holds for all the verbal or oral gifts. Therefore, the person may speak in tongues whenever he chooses. By the same token he can control himself in ceasing to speak in tongues whenever he chooses (see I Corinthians 14:32).

Paul summed it up when he said the he can and therefore *will* pray in tongues whenever he decides. Also, he will pray with his mind, or intelligence, whenever he pleases. The word 'will' expresses decision or determination in the act. 'I will' implies the freedom to speak in this case. Praying with his 'mind' means praying in his native language (see I Corinthians 14:15).

A person who has received the baptism with the Holy Spirit has the privilege of "praying in the spirit [tongues] on all occasions with all kinds of prayers and requests" (Ephesians 6:18). We are encouraged to pray in both modes, mind and spirit.

QUESTION 15: If we each have a gift, and if everyone of us should exercise it once we realize what it is, could it be that some of us hinder the exercise of someone else's gift by either standing in the way or by doing too much in the church? How should leadership handle the placing of persons who feel that they know what their gifts are?

ANSWER: Good question! In many churches, particularly the smaller ones, a few people seem to have most of the jobs and are simply overworked. This may be due in part to others who will not become active or function in any given capacity.

It has been said that if you want someone to do a job, ask a busy person to do it. Generally, he/she will carry out the task. But isn't this unfair? Some church members become overworked while others are denied training for work in the church. Finally, some able members may suffer burnout and quit. Then, we might be tempted to call them 'backsliders.' We must change our thinking about church work. We must reconcile the role of gifts in the church and place people where they function best with their gifts.

However, we should point out that we do not hinder a particular person from manifesting his gift if he will not take responsibility for it in the first place. Christians should be taught about the gifts of the Spirit and be encouraged to discover their gifts and function in the church. When we speak of gifts we refer to all the gifts of the Spirit—30 or more, possibly (see Romans 12:3-8; Ephesians 4:11; and I Corinthians 12:7-10).

Those in positions of leadership have the duty to teach and encourage their people to discover their gifts, to work with them, and to place them in the church body so that they may function smoothly and properly. In so doing, the various tasks and outreach of the church may be more easily carried out.

Leadership and the people concerned should feel free to experiment and work together in this undertaking until each one has found his or her place of service. At the same time this 'job placement' relieves personnel in places of leadership who are overworked.

When a person discovers her gift, she can feel comfortable with it. Commitment can then more freely come about. Too long have we put people in the wrong jobs. And then we are surprised when they do not become committed. We do not understand why they quit. We must be careful not to place 'square pegs in round holes,' or vice-versa.

QUESTION 16: What did Jesus mean in John 20:22 when "He breathed on them, and said, 'Receive the Holy Spirit?'

ANSWER: This is acknowledged to be a controversial

Questions and Answers

passage, and consequently different interpretations have been given. However, several things must be remembered as we look into the text.

I, along with others, do not believe that the Spirit was given at the time Jesus made this statement. The term, "breathed on them," may be translated as, "He inspired them," in the sense that He encouraged them to wait for the Promise of the Father (Acts 1:15). If indeed the Holy Spirit had been given in the Johannine passage that you are referring to, Pentecost would have been pre-empted, and therefore pointless. This could not be.

Pentecost is known universally by all Church historians and scholars to be the birthday of the Church. The Church Age was ushered in with a great display of heavenly fanfare and fireworks including the reverberation of a violent wind. This demonstrated and signified that Jesus had been glorified (John 7:37), the dispensation of the Law terminated, and the Day of Grace begun. This would be an event the disciples and the Church would always remember and to which they would always refer (see Acts 11:15).

There is only one giving of the Spirit in the New Testament, and that was on the Day of Pentecost. The Spirit could not be given until Jesus had been glorified (John 7:37).

We believe that the passage in John corresponds to the passages in Matthew: 28:18-20; Mark 16:16, 17; and Luke 24:49-53. They are to be understood as being futuristic from the time spoken. This understanding harmonizes Scripture.

Jacob H. Stern says, "Yeshua's [Jesus] breathing was meaningful—but symbolic. The *Talmidim* [disciples] actually received the Holy Spirit's power a month-and-a-half later, at *Shavu'ot* [Pentecost]."[70]

QUESTION 17: Please explain Romans 8:26 and 27,
> In the same way, the Spirit helps us in our weakness. We do not know what we ought to pray, but the Spirit himself intercedes for us with groans

that words cannot express. And he who searches our hearts knows the mind of the Spirit, because the Spirit intercedes for the saints in accordance with God's will.

ANSWER: We do not always know the will of God in every matter about which we pray. Also, we may be prejudiced in our minds, biased, or even selfish as to how we pray and what we pray for. But, we can pray in the Spirit [tongues] and feel that we are praying in the direct will of God. The Spirit makes intercession for us. He knows our minds and the mind of the Father as well.

The Spirit pleads on our behalf with "unspeakable yearnings and groanings too deep for utterance" (AMP). It is generally agreed that this passage refers to praying in tongues. In the context of I Corinthians 14:15, "praying in the Spirit" means 'tongues.' The term is used in other passages as well (see Jude 20; and Ephesians 6:18).

To be logically consistent, the term should mean the same wherever it is found in the Bible. This being the case, we may say that Paul commanded us to pray in tongues! In Ephesians 6:18 he said, "Pray in the Spirit on all occasions with all kinds of prayers and requests."

Simply put, this means that we may come to God in prayer and make our needs known intelligently [mind] and then pray in the Spirit [tongues] for the same requests. We can and should pray both ways.

This command was given because we have the ability to carry it out. We see this possibility in Romans 8:26, and 27. This is another good reason that a person should desire to manifest the Holy Spirit.

QUESTION 18: If a person has been filled with the Holy Spirit for years and is still hanging on to his old habits of the world such as drinking, abusing drugs, smoking, etc., or he believes that it is alright to do these things, should that person be placed in a position of leadership? If people are told that they can continue these habits and still make it to heaven, why give them [the habits] up?

ANSWER: In response to the first question: each church or group determines the qualifications for leadership within that particular group. I belong to a church that has determined that persons in leadership positions should not drink, smoke, use drugs, etc. But I cannot dictate my personal beliefs to another group to which I do not belong, and which may have differing opinions on these issues.

It may be better that we do not judge other Christians, for we do not stand or fall before one another. We all stand or fall before God alone (Romans 14:4). As to another who is not of our group, "God is able to make him stand."

However, a drug abuser should have no place of leadership in any Christian group. This would hold for sexual deviants as well (see Galatians 5:19-21 and Colossians 3:5-7). Living in a state of sinful activity should not be tolerated among those considered to be role models for others.

Why give up the habits? Surely not just to go to heaven. Nor for purely legalistic reasons. If a person gave these things up just so he could go to heaven, he apparently missed the point of the Christian faith. Many people who are not Christians do not drink, smoke, or use drugs. They still are not going to heaven because they have not accepted Christ's sacrifice for their sins.

One must place his faith in the regenerative work of the cross to gain salvation and heaven. Having done so, he should desire to please his Savior. He willingly follows Paul's word,

> Let us throw off everything that hinders and the sin that so easily entangles, and let us run with perseverance the race marked out for us. Let us fix our eyes on Jesus, the pioneer and perfecter of our faith (Hebrews 12:1).

As a person matures in Christ and follows the leading of

the Holy Spirit and the dictates of his renewed conscience, he then may begin to lay aside many things [habits, and even personal desires] that could hinder his walk with God or mar his Christian testimony. Paul handles this well in Romans 14.

After all, it is the normal state of the Christian to want to please the Lord. We have known many people to give up these habits after having received the filling with the Holy Spirit. They normally do not 'count the cost' of following Him. He enables them to "strive for perfection out of reverence for God" (II Corinthians 7:1).

QUESTION 19: When we pray in tongues, can Satan understand our prayer?

ANSWER: We must not worry about Satan's knowledge, for God has him in check. We believe that 'unknown tongues' are languages known somewhere in the world; they are unknown only to the native speaker of the tongue. In Acts 2:1-4 the Jews had gathered at Pentecost from all over the Roman Empire, "And they were confounded because each one heard them speaking in his own language [dialect]" (Acts 2:6). The disciples were speaking in other tongues, but they were not unknown to the hearers. Other people understood the languages.

Satan cannot read your mind! He is not omniscient or all knowing. Anything not spoken is private and concealed from everyone but God, for He alone knows our thoughts. Satan cannot invade the believer's privacy, for "greater is he that is in you, than he that is in the world" (I John 4:4 KJV).

No, Satan cannot read our minds. However, his temptations and our spiritual battles take place in the mind. But God's protection is ever present. We must not succumb to paranoia of fear and distrust. Trust in God allays all fear (see Luke 11:13).

QUESTION 20: People who speak against tongues argue that it should not be done because Jesus never spoke in tongues. How do you answer that?

ANSWER: Jesus was a man of His times as were the disciples and even the Old Testament saints. "Up to that time [Pentecost], the Spirit had not been given, since Jesus had not yet been glorified" (John 7:39). Hence, there were no tongues as of yet. The era of the Spirit, or Church Age, began at Pentecost with the outpouring of the Spirit. Then men began to speak with tongues (Acts 2:1-4).

Jesus is Deity, "for in Christ all the fullness of the Deity lives in bodily form" (Colossians 2:9). And, "God was pleased to have all his fullness dwell in him" (Colossians 1:19). Being Deity, there was no necessity for the Holy Spirit to intercede for Him as for us (see Romans 8:26, 27).

Jesus embodied the Holy Spirit. When He died on the cross and returned to the Father, having been glorified, He released the Spirit to the entire world. For He had said, "It is for your good that I am going away. Unless I go away, the Counselor will not come to you; but if I go, I will send him to you." (John 16:7) Therefore, tongues are for us—not for Jesus.

QUESTION 21: Is there any language that is unknown?

ANSWER: I do not think so. Paul said, "Undoubtedly there are all sorts of languages in the world, yet none of them is without meaning" (I Corinthians 14:10).

The Linguistics Institute in San Antonio, Texas, stated that there are about 10,000 languages and dialects in the world. Another study states that there are about 7,010 languages and dialects in the world. About 3,000 languages have been translated. Furthermore, the Institute said it would take another twenty years per language to translate these remaining 3,000 languages. The tongues spoken at Pentecost were languages known and spoken in the Roman Empire. The tongues in I Corinthians 14 were known languages.

Also, the word "unknown" is not used in the original Greek text. There are no "unknown" tongues. They are called "other tongues." Tongues are unknown only to the speaker. The King James Version inserts the word "unknown," but it is not in the original manuscript. You will notice that it is in italics (I Corinthians 14:2, 4, 13, 14, 19, and 27). This means that it was an interpretive addition to the text. To be consistent with Acts 2:4-11 we must conclude that when one speaks in tongues he is praising God or praying in a language known by someone somewhere in the world.

QUESTION 22: In I Corinthians 13:1, Paul said, "If I speak in the tongues of men and of angels, but have not love, I am only a resounding gong or a clanging cymbal." What do you make of this?

ANSWER: In this passage Paul spoke in the subjunctive case, in hyperbole, only to prove the point that love is superior to the spiritual gifts. However, love is not a gift of the Spirit. He did not suggest that there are angelic tongues, or that there is a possibility of speaking with angels' tongues. We do not know how angels converse or communicate. He simply stated that, even if it were possible to speak in an angelic language, but did not have love, it would not profit him.

In this chapter Paul was making the case for the fruit of the Spirit—LOVE—as being far superior to the ostentatious spiritual gifts. The Corinthians were esteeming these gifts so highly—too highly—to the neglect of Christian love. The spiritual gifts are for the here-and-now, but love is for eternity. 'Tongues,' as such, is not the subject of the passage. Love is the subject.

QUESTION 23: Must one be baptized in water before one may be baptized or filled with the Holy Spirit?

ANSWER: No. In Acts 10 we read the conversion story of Cornelius, the Centurion. The Gentiles believed and accepted the Gospel message in their hearts while Peter was preaching. God honored their faith by baptizing them with the Spirit. The Apostle baptized them in water soon after the experience.

Peter asked the Jewish brethren who had come with him, "Can anyone keep these people from being baptized with water? They have received the Holy Spirit just as we have. So he ordered that they be baptized in the name of Jesus Christ" (10:47 and 48).

Note, Peter "ordered that they be baptized..." Christians should follow the Lord in water baptism as soon as possible, either before, or after, the tongues experience. They did so immediately upon conversion in the New Testament (see Act 2:38, 39 and Romans 6:1-4.)

Lest a person think that water baptism is unimportant, we remind him that in His Great Commission Jesus commanded us to baptize (Matthew 28:19). Therefore, it is important. It is one of the sacraments, or ordinances, of the Church, the other being Holy Communion. However, the sequence is not relevant. Manifesting the Spirit may come before or after water baptism.

QUESTION 24: Why do you tell those who are seeking to manifest the Holy Spirit to repeat words from your own prayer language? Was this to help them break through their resistance to speaking in tongues? If only repetition of your words was spoken, is this a valid initial evidence of tongues for those instructed?

ANSWER: Laurence Christensen, the noted Lutheran Charismatic churchman, has said that a person may be coached into speaking in tongues, but he cannot be coached into continuing to speak in tongues.

I instruct speakers to 'follow me in the Spirit.' That is, when I pray in the Spirit, they should join me in prayer and start speaking out—not in English—or any other acquired language. This enables the person to 'let go' and get in the flow of the Spirit. He soon senses God's presence, the Spirit moves upon him, and he realizes that he can manifest the gift and does so readily and with ease.

This is valid initial evidence of tongues. Christensen has also advised us that it does not matter that a person has been coached into speaking with tongues. But he cannot be coached forever after. If he has a valid experience, it will prove itself effective.

Oral Roberts has been instrumental in helping people receive Spirit baptism with speaking in tongues. He advises those who desire the experience of tongues to get with those who are praying in tongues and make the start themselves [i.e., initiate the action] by joining in with them. In such action God moves within the person and gives him his own prayer language.

Dennis Bennett practiced this methodology in the first transdenominational Holy Spirit conference for the Assemblies of God in Springfield, Missouri in 1982. On that occasion about 125 believers manifested the Spirit.

I use the terms 'receive the baptism in the Spirit,' and 'manifest the Spirit' interchangeably here so as not to confuse traditional Pentecostals who prefer the former term, and the rest of us who prefer the term 'manifest.' We realize that we have already received the Spirit. I refer to the one and same experience. They are equally good terms.

We have followed this method and practice with considerable success. Over 19,450 people have received their baptism—the tongues experience—in our meetings around the world as they have prayerfully taken our advice.

We also advise people to actively engage in the manifestation of the Spirit. God gives the Gift as the person accepts it as an act of faith in verbalizing it. God does not force anyone to speak with tongues, but if a person desires the experience and will of his own volition speak out when prayer is offered, the Spirit will enable the person to speak in tongues.

QUESTION 25: Why should I desire to speak with

tongues?

ANSWER: When this question is asked, one of two things is usually evident. Either the inquirer doe not realize that he resists the fullness of the Holy Spirit, or he simply does not know or understand the Scriptures on the subject. Maybe both. Let's clear it up.

(1) Paul made three important statements in I Corinthian 14 that we may consider:
    (a) I would like every one of you to speak in tongues…(14:5).
    (b) I thank God that I speak in tongues more than all of you (14:18).
    (c) He who speaks in a tongue edifies himself (14:4).

This is the only gift given in which it is said that one edifies *himself* by the practice of it. Think of it…it must be valuable! I believe that by practicing this Gift one is built up in that area of life and person which is in the greatest spiritual need at that time.

(2) Tongues increase the possibility of a deepened prayer life. Paul said, "Pray in the Spirit on all occasions with all kinds of prayers and requests" (Ephesians 6:18).

(3) Tongues is one of the gifts of the Spirit. Historically and biblically it is the initial evidence of having received the baptism with the Spirit.

(4) We are told to desire spiritual gifts (I Corinthians 14:1). These are only a few of the reasons why one should desire to speak with tongues. An interesting side point: have you ever heard of someone who manifested the Spirit who regretted it?

QUESTION 26: Why do the Pentecostal churches put so much emphasis on tongues when it is the 'least' of the gifts? I praise God that I speak with tongues; however, there is so much more. We appear to get hung up on tongues. We should seek the power, not the tongues.

ANSWER: First, I disagree that we do get 'hung up' on tongues. According to a survey previously referred to, perhaps as many as fifty percent of the people in the Pentecostal/Charismatic churches do not, or have not, spoken in tongues. Furthermore, some apparently do not care to do so. This is significant in light of the fact that Pentecostals and Charismatics have earned their reputation from their concentration on tongues healing, and miracles, etc.

Secondly, tongues has been mislabeled as the 'least' of the gifts of the Spirit. This is an arbitrary pronouncement without validity. All the gifts are equally valid and important in their place and function. The Bible never indicates tongues to be unimportant or inferior to the other gifts.

Tongues with interpretation serve along with prophecy to edify the church (I Corinthians 14:26-32). The Bible also says, "Do not treat prophecies with contempt: (I Thessalonians 5:20). "Be eager to prophecy, and do not forbid speaking in tongues" (I Corinthians 14:39).

Of course there is more to it than tongues, but the baptism with the Hoy Spirit with the speaking in tongues is the gateway to many greater experiences with God. We must go through the gate, not around it. And we must remember that while some have the Gift plus others, we are always in the process of teaching those who are new to the faith and who are seeking. Some of us then must be patient and let them learn for the first time while we are strengthened by earning and re-enforcement.

It may be that we are not to seek power for its own sake, but to deny that we want power for the Gospel's sake is absurd. When under persecution, the disciples prayed:

> Now, Lord, consider their threats and enable your
> servants to speak your word with great boldness.
> Stretch out your hand to heal and perform mirac-
> ulous signs and wonders through the name of

your holy servant Jesus (Acts 4:29, 30).

There is no power without turning on the switch. We need only to be filled with the Spirit to realize the power He has provided for every occasion. We are not 'hung up' on tongues. Rather, many may be hung up on how to receive their gift. Others are hung up in their bias against the spiritual gifts. We are trying to remove the hang-ups.

QUESTION 27: I have received the baptism with the Holy Spirit and spoke in tongues at the time. I have not been able to pray in tongues since. Why is this?

ANSWER: I suspect that this may be due to a misunderstanding on your part. Speaking with tongues is not usually an automatic act that God performs 'on' people. A person cannot be in a passive frame of mind or mood and expect God to impel him or her to speak in tongues. This would violate a person's personality and will. God does not usually act in this manner.

To speak in tongues initially or thereafter, one must speak willfully. The principle of I Corinthians 14:32 is the key: "The spirits of prophets are subject to the control of prophets." This holds for all the verbal or oral gifts. The speaker in tongues can, therefore, speak in tongues at will. Try it. You might like it.

When you do initiate the speaking in tongues you may be tempted to feel that it is not 'real' because you feel you have 'caused' it, or brought it about. "That is just *me*," you might think. You may feel you are making it up or that it is mere gibberish. These are some of Satan's one-liners used to discourage you.

Instead, accept by faith that it *is* real and in time it will take on meaning for you spiritually and emotionally. A great number of people have reported back to me that it has.

QUESTION 28: It is said that the Holy Spirit works in a gentlemanly fashion. Would He give a word of knowledge to someone whose heart it would disturb or trouble?

ANSWER: Privately, he might do so. Jesus revealed to the woman at the well things in her past that could only be known by a word of knowledge (John 4:16-20). This may have troubled her at first, but it brought her to salvation and faith in Jesus.

We see it in the story of Gehazi and Naaman the Leper (II Kings 5). When Elisha's servant, Gehazi, wrongfully took the silver and the garments from the Syrian general in payment for his healing, Elisha confronted him privately, but sternly, with his sin by a word of knowledge. He said, "Was not my spirit with you when the man got down from his chariot to meet you?" (5:26). As a result of this knowledge, Gehazi's sin was uncovered and he was severely punished by becoming a leper himself.

Peter, by a word of knowledge, revealed Ananias' and Saphira's sin in lying to the Holy Spirit. His announcement was a public revelation and confrontation that resulted in their deaths. Sin is after all a dangerous game (Acts 5). The gifts, properly used, are given to keep the Church holy.

It appears that if a matter is of a private nature, God deals in a private manner. If public, God goes public! In private cases, the Gift is used to enable a person to get right with God. In the public demonstration, God intercedes to safeguard His honor, character, and integrity.

We need not fear that the Holy Spirit is going to intentionally embarrass someone by another's [gifted person] foolish demonstration in the church. Also, we need not fear that someone can read our minds and reveal our faults and foibles. God is too gracious to allow this.

The gifts of the Spirit are given to aid the Church in a supernatural manner and to keep it pure. He will deal kindly with His people to draw them closer to Him.

QUESTION 29: Why is it that some people have a jubilant and strong experience when they manifest the Holy Spirit, while others struggle with it and even sometimes doubt whether or not they have ever received it?

ANSWER: There appears to be two groups of people who respond in two different ways to the 'tongues' phenomenon. On the one hand, some people have a great desire to manifest the Spirit. When prayer is offered, they immediately 'enter-in' with all their hearts and put all they have into the experience. They approach the Throne with great expectancy and desire. They worship freely, expressing their praise aloud to the Lord. They voluntarily enter into adoration and worship. They exercise faith in the Promise of God. This cooperation with the Lord enables them to receive or manifest the Spirit freely and often emotionally. They are expecting the blessing, and by faith they open up to it.

On the other hand, some struggle because they have little expectancy, or do not fully realize that they must cooperate with the Spirit in the manifestation. Some people, at the time of prayer, rather than entering into worship and praise, try to mentally analyze the operation of the Spirit. Some try to conjure up an experience, trying to figure it out or understand it. They try to ascertain the moving of the Spirit subjectively. This hinders them in manifesting the Spirit.

To manifest the Spirit joyfully with a good strong experience, one should examine the Scriptures. He should ascertain for himself that the experience is meant for him and that God wills it for him. He may then ask God for it, expect and experience it! He should memorize Luke 11:13:

> If you then, though you are evil, know how to give good gifts to your children, how much more will your Father in heaven give the Holy Spirit to those who ask him? Believe it, accept it, and begin to worship and adore the Lord Jesus aloud.

Praise is the key to being filled with the Spirit.

We encourage the one who seems to get a weak start in the manifestation to believe that his experience is real. He will receive an emotional lift in time. He can become cheerful and joyful with a strong and firm experience as he gives himself to worship and praise. He should not deny, or denigrate the work begun in his life because of lack of emotion. Neither should he compare himself and his experience to that of another person. Thanksgiving opens the arms and heart of God. Let us learn to praise.

QUESTION 30: Please explain Acts 4:31 in light of Acts 2:4.

> After they prayed, the place where they were meeting was shaken. And they were all filled with the Holy Spirit and spoke the word of God boldly (Acts 4:31).
>
> All of them were filled with the Holy Spirit and began to speak in other tongues as the Spirit enabled them (Acts 2:4)

ANSWER: The term, "filled" connotes the idea of 'control' by the Spirit. In both texts they were "filled" with the Spirit. That is, they were controlled, grasped, or seized by the Spirit. They took action. They *did* something.

In the former instance "they began to speak in tongues," while in the latter case they spoke boldly or preached the Word. To be filled, controlled, guided, or led by the Spirit connotes the idea of subsequent action as a result.

With the baptism with the Holy Spirit, the initial evidence of speaking with tongues is seen to be the normative, observable, and objective evidence that a person has manifested the Spirit's presence. It is the criterion by which the experience can be judged.

The new believer has had no time for fruit bearing, yet the church can know that he has manifested the Spirit. Tongues are that evidence (see Acts 10:44-46 and 11:15-18).

Subsequent to regeneration, the idea of being filled [controlled] is seen in fruit bearing and action for the Gospel of Jesus Christ. "By their fruit you will recognize them" (Matthew 7:16) is now the criterion evidencing the fact that one has been filled. A fruit-bearing Christian is one who is led by the Spirit and lives under the Spirit's control and leadership.

In Acts 2 they were filled and spoke in tongues. In Acts 4 they were filled and spoke the Word of God boldly. When a Christian is filled, he/she takes action.

QUESTION 31: If the baptism with the Holy Spirit [tongues manifestation] comes from within the believer, then what do the following expressions mean?

> ...tarry...until ye be endued with power from on high (Luke 24:49 KJV).
>
> I will pour out my Spirit upon all flesh" (cf. Joel 2:28 with Acts 2:17 KJV).
>
> The Holy Ghost fell on all of them...On the Gentiles also was poured out the gift of the Holy Ghost (Acts 10:44 and 45 KJV).
>
> The Holy Ghost came on them..." (Acts 19:6 KJV).

ANSWER: In Luke 24:49 the word "endued" should be translated to read, "clothed." The word "from" refers to the giving of the Spirit from God on high at Pentecost. The Spirit comes into the heart of the believer when he comes to Christ, and flows from within the person when he manifests his Spirit baptism (see John 7:37-39).

The baptism with the Spirit is seen to be a two-phase event or a sequence in a double event. The Spirit comes into the heart of a person at the time of salvation and he is subsequently filled from within, or baptized with the Spirit, when he releases the Spirit from within. "From his heart shall flow rivers of living water..." (John 7:38). The manifestation comes from within.

In Acts 2:17, "pour out" means to give or bestow the Spirit. This is a metaphorical term. He cannot be literally "poured out" for He is a person. But He can be given.

In Acts 10:44, "fell on all them," and "came upon all" (NIV) means that He seized, grasped or overwhelmed them—another metaphorical phrase.

In Acts 10:45 "poured out" means He is given or imparted.

The words endued (clothed), *came upon, fell upon*, etc., are simply words that denote control by the Holy Spirit. Some cognate terms might mean that the Holy Spirit grasped them, or seized them. In modern terminology we could say that the Holy Spirit 'grabbed' them. These New Testament terms should be translated into our modern day speech if the laity is to understand them fully and correctly.

When a person is saved, he receives the Holy Spirit (see Romans 8:9 and I Corinthians 6:19 and 12:13). He is born from above (John 3:3). When he manifests the Spirit, the manifestation comes from within the person. "Out of his heart [belly, innermost being, from within] shall flow rivers of living water. But this spoke he of the Spirit" (John 7:37-39). The manifestation does not come from above and down into the person. Rather, the blessing comes from within the person, up and out in the speaking in tongues.

The Israelites in the desert drank from the Rock that accompanied them (I Corinthians 10:4). The Christian drinks from the Rock that is within him. Praise God. He need never be thirsty again. Jesus said, "The water I give him will become in him a spring of water welling up to everlasting life" (John 4:14).

The manifestation of tongues comes from within the spirit of the born-again, baptized-in-the-Spirit child of God. As Paul said, "My spirit prays" (I Corinthians 14:14). The power comes 'upon' one, or is available to one when he is especially anointed by the Holy Spirit to perform a particular task or to witness for Christ. Also, this is a resident power that each believer possesses for service. He can draw upon this resident ***dunamis*** (potential power) whenever needed. *Dunamis* must become *energeia* (flowing energy) if we are to be effective witnesses for Christ.[71]

To be endued with power means to be clothed with power. For God to pour out His Spirit means that God gives His Spirit to His people. The term 'power' conveys the idea of ability or authority to live and witness for Christ in this context.

QUESTION 32: Please explain the gift of prophecy, divers kinds of tongues, and interpretation of tongues. How do we receive these gifts?

ANSWER: The manifestation gifts in question are three of the nine gifts listed in I Corinthians 12:7-10.

The gift of prophecy is manifested when a person gives a message publicly in the assembly in the native language of that people. It is a message heard in their own tongue by one who speaks their language. No interpretation is needed, for it is readily and easily understood by the church. To prophesy means to speak God's message to mankind.

It is a message of "edification, exhortation and comfort" (I Corinthians 14:3 KJV). It is given to aid, assist, to lift the believer up and to draw him nearer to God. It is not negative, nor condemnatory, but rather a positive helpful message. It is given to encourage.

Divers [various] kinds of tongues are manifested when a person speaks aloud publicly in the assembly in another tongue other than that of the native language of the people. We have erroneously called it an 'unknown' tongue. The term 'unknown tongue' is not used in the Greek text. The term, 'other' is correct. The speaker or the church does not understand this tongue or language. The gift of interpretation of tongues must accompany the gift of tongues for the church's comprehension and edification (see I Corinthians 14:13, 27, and 28).

Interpretation of tongues is a gift of the Spirit just as are prophecy and the gift of tongues. When a person speaks publicly in tongues, there must be an interpreter in the church (i.e., one who has the gift of interpretation of tongues). If there is no interpreter in the church, the speaker in tongues must remain silent, or "pray that he may interpret" himself (I Corinthians 14:13).

In our seminars we have told our people that if anyone speaks in tongues (i.e., gives a message), and no one interprets the message, he has the responsibility of interpreting it himself! Perhaps it is better for one to manifest the gifts in his own home church, for then he would know whether there is an interpreter present in the church.

This causes some who speak in tongues to think twice before speaking, because they may end up having to interpret their own messages. They are generally more fearful of interpreting than they are of speaking in tongues, for when one speaks in the native language, he has to take care to speak sensibly and scripturally. The speaker in tongues does not ordinarily concern himself with this aspect.

We feel that those who manifest these gifts, or are used by the Spirit in these demonstrations, ought to have a basic biblical knowledge and be close to the church. Some churches require this for good reasons. First, if one does not know basic biblical doctrine and Scripture, he may interpret a tongue, or he may prophecy inaccurately. It does not necessarily mean that the speaker is in 'the flesh,' or living in sin or out of touch with God. It may only mean that he does not fully know what he is talking about. After all, we do speak within the limits of our knowledge. In the inspiration of the moment, he may have gone beyond his ability to perform. The Apostle realized this possibility when he said, "If a man's gift is prophesying let him use it in proportion to his faith" (Romans 12:6).

Second, it should be required that one who participates in the manifestation gifts be a member of that body, or at least be well known by the group. They can ascertain his daily living and moral conduct.

Since the manifestations in question are gifts of the Spirit, we are not urged to request them. The Holy Spirit "gives them to each one, just as he determines" (I Corinthians 12:11). We must, however, set out to discern what our gifts are, and this is done by experimentation. As Peter Wagner has said in his Church Growth lectures at Fuller Theological Seminary, "we must discover our gifts, or gift-mix." As someone has said (in another context), "Try it, you might like it."

One must find out for himself how he fits into the scheme of things—what gifts work for him, or where he feels comfortable. I know of one large church that makes time after a Sunday evening service for those who wish to practice the manifestation gifts. It seems to work and is also edifying to the church body.

When we discover our gifts, we then must set out to learn how to use them or manifest them properly in the context of the local church. It would be helpful if all Pentecostal/Charismatic churches had training sessions for their people in the manifestation gifts. Some do. We encourage these and often assist in this training.

QUESTION 33: Please explain how I, a Spirit-filled, baptized believer, went through deliverance of evil spirits, and how my wife also went through the same.

ANSWER: The answer to this one is complex. I do not know the circumstances or the occasion to which you refer. Also, there is much misunderstanding and confusion on this subject among our people. First, let me say that I do not subscribe to the teaching that Christians can be demon-possessed. The Scriptures do not indicate this possibility. There are no examples of exorcism of a ***Christian*** in the Bible.

Jesus and the apostles cast out demons to set people free from sin and the bondage of Satan. This was a sign of the coming kingdom that resulted in people being converted to Jesus.

In Mark 16:17 and 18, we note that the Church shall have power to cast out demons and heal the sick. These signs validate the claims of Jesus as the Messiah, and enhance His proclamation. The name of Jesus is exalted by these signs and wonders. Healing the sick, speaking with new tongues, and casting out demons is an integral part of the Great Commission to "Go ye into all the world..." (Matthew 28:19, 20 and Mark 16:15-18).

We are to use these gifts to proclaim the Gospel and set free a bound world. God's people have been set free by the Word, cleansed by the Blood of the Lamb, and have received the Holy Spirit, which is a guarantee of their inheritance of eternal life. Therefore, we do not exorcise demons from other believers in the Church, nor do we cast out any foreign spirit from them.

We must also remember that we have the Comforter, the Holy Spirit, who abides within the heart of the believer. Jesus said, "And I will ask the Father, and he will give you another Counselor to be with you forever—the Spirit of truth" (John 14:16).

The Bible says, "The one who is in you is greater than the one [Satanic or demonic spirit] who is in the world" (I John 4:4). This is the guarantee of our security and protection in the Lord Jesus Christ. We can safely trust the Lord Jesus to take care of us. Thus, we need not fear Satan, or his demonic spirits. The Christian is safe in the arms of Jesus.

If Jesus cannot protect us from demonic possession, He cannot save us ultimately. Paul said, "I know whom I have believed, and am convinced that he is able to guard what I have entrusted [my soul, works, etc.] to him for that day" (II Timothy 1:12).

A Christian may have physical or mental illness and frustrations. He or she may be in need of pastoral care and counseling at times, but this is not to be confused with demonism or possession. Perhaps you and your wife were delivered from some of these other situations. A Christian may be *oppressed* by the enemy at times or have mental problems and need deliverance, but this is not to be confused with demonic *possession*.

QUESTION 34: Is speaking in tongues a gift or a manifestation of the Spirit? If it is a gift, I understand that God will not take it away from a person. If it is a manifestation, the how can the Holy Spirit be manifested in someone who is a backslider?

ANSWER: Let us put it this way: The Holy Spirit is a gift. We receive "the gift of the Holy Spirit" (Acts 2:38). Tongues are a manifestation of the gift and is received or manifested at the time a person is baptized with the Holy Spirit (Acts 2:4). This is devotional tongues, which are to be exercised in one's private prayer life. The Scripture declares that "God's gifts and his call are irrevocable" (Romans 11:29). That is, God's purposes and God's gifts will stand as given.

There is also the gift of tongues listed with the gifts of the Spirit (I Corinthians 12:7-11). While it is called a gift, it is also called a manifestation. In the Greek text the gifts are called "spirituals."

That God can, and at times does, manifest Himself in unholy persons or backsliders, must be recognized and acknowledged. Yet this must not confuse us as to their personal piety and devotion to God. We see it in the Bible repeatedly. "Is Saul among the prophets" was a proverb in Israel (I Samuel 10:12 and 19:24). Saul fell away from God, yet could manifest a prophetic utterance.

Pentecostal pastors have long realized that backsliders can talk in tongues, for it is their gift. "For if I pray in a tongue, my spirit prays," said Paul (I Corinthians 14:14). This ability is not rescinded because of a lapse in the moral conduct or condition of the person involved.

We know of a case in which a person backslid and returned to the bars and a drunken lifestyle. While in a state of intoxication he would speak in tongues. He was aware of it, and it brought him under great conviction, and eventually to a re-commitment of his life to Jesus Christ. Admittedly this is an unusual incident.

I pastored a church in which a man and his wife from outside the community visited us on occasion. We were always happy to have them visit us, for one would give a message in tongues and the other could interpret. One of them would prophesy with great power. It was inspirational.

Years later, after I had left the church, I learned that the couple had been living a life of immorality at the time. Yet they could be used in the gifts.

But they had been members of the church I pastored. Had I known the facts of their lives at the time, I would not have permitted them to move in the gifts of the Spirit in the assembly of believers. Had the community known about their personal lives, the church would have lost credibility. People who get involved in the spiritual gifts should be members of the church, or at least be known to the church so that their character may be known.

So we must realize that tongues, or any of the gifts of the Spirit are not indicative of true spirituality, or being Spirit-filled, The fruit of the Spirit is the test of spirituality and the Spirit-led life. "Thus, by their fruit you will recognize them" (Matthew 7:20) is the test.

QUESTION 35: I believe the Holy Spirit is received at salvation. Then what is the baptism with the Holy Spirit? In simple language, what is it?

ANSWER: The religion editor of the San Diego Union-Tribune put that question to me bluntly in a personal interview some time ago. Here was my answer, then and now. The baptism with the Holy Spirit is the reception of the

Spirit, which results in the person being able to manifest His presence with the speaking in tongues.

In the Book of Acts the earliest history of the New Testament Church, we note than on every occasion when people came to Christ, they immediately spoke with tongues. In Acts 10 and 11 it was the manifestation of tongues that indicated to the Jewish Church at Jerusalem that the Gentiles had received the Holy Spirit and were, therefore, to be accepted as co-believers in Jesus Christ.

Put simply, the baptism with the Spirit is the reception of the Spirit with the resulting manifestation of tongues. The fact that not all who make a profession of faith in Jesus manifest the Spirit with tongues does not mean that they cannot. It only means that they have not, for some reason or other. With proper understanding, any Christian can speak in tongues if he or she wishes. We are trying to help believers understand this (Acts 2:4; 10, 11, and 19:1-6).

QUESTION 36: Can children receive the baptism with the Holy Spirit? Can they speak in tongues?

ANSWER: Yes, they certainly do. Children can and do receive the baptism with the Holy Spirit, and they speak with tongues just as adults do.

In my book, *Pentecost in the Pentagon*, I related the story of a five-year-old girl who manifested the Spirit in our meeting. She was a precocious child having accepted Jesus as Lord of her life at the age of three. I gave the invitation for those who desired prayer and the laying on of hands to rise and come forward. She stood and made her way to the altar with many adults who desired the blessing.

At the time, I felt that she was too young to understand or comprehend what was happening. I simply prayed for her in a perfunctory manner by placing my hands on her head and asked God to fill her with the Spirit. I quickly left her to pray for the adults, whereupon she raised her arms to heaven and began to speak with tongues.

The pastor told me years later that this girl served God all through her school years and at the time I wrote the book she was a "radiant senior in high school living for Jesus Christ." Since that time we have seen hundreds of children manifest the "Spirit with the attending phenomenon of speaking in tongues.

QUESTION 37: How can we receive the power to heal someone through the laying on of hands?

ANSWER: "[The Spirit] gives them [gifts] to each man, just as he determines" (I Corinthians 12:11). The gifts are resident in the Holy Spirit who determines whether or not you will have the gift of healing.

God's people are given different gifts so that in any one given church body, we all may function as the members of the Church Body, Christ being the Head (I Corinthians 12, cf. Ephesians 4:15 and 16). As members we make up the functioning body; therefore we are all needed.

We do not all have the gift of healing but we are required to pray for the sick as the occasion mandates (see James 5:13-16). However, we should not develop a guilt complex if a person is not healed After all, God is sovereign in the affairs of men. He heals whom He will, and when He will. Therefore, the Church must resist a negative attitude and a guilt complex due to what we often consider 'failure' for unanswered prayer concerning anyone's healing.

However, the members of the body realize that they are all gifted people. As each one discovers his/her gift, all can function in the body with it. Then healings as well as miracles may occur on a more frequent basis. We should not seek the ostentatious gifts. Let us be satisfied with the gifts with which the Spirit endows us.

QUESTION 38: Please explain the gift of the Word of Knowledge and how it is received.

ANSWER: The Word of Knowledge is one of the gifts of the Spirit listed in I Corinthians 12:7-10. It is known to be in operation when something is revealed to a person concerning another's activities or motivation in relation to God.

A prime example is that of Ananias and Saphira (Acts 5). The believers had agreed to sell their properties and divide it equally to share with those who had need. This was a voluntary act, and apparently no command had been given by the Lord to do it. Therefore no one was compelled to enter into the agreement. But once a person agreed to the arrangement, honesty was of course mandated.

Ananias and his wife sold a piece of property and pretended to present all of the proceeds to the apostles for distribution. In truth they only gave a small portion of the proceeds to the apostles. Since the action was to be a voluntary one, there was no need to deceive.

A Word of Knowledge made their act of deceit known to the apostle Peter. The Spirit revealed the deception to him. He confronted Ananias and Saphira separately about the transaction. In a prearranged agreement between themselves, they lied. At the moment of confrontation they both died because of their sin. As a result, "great fear seized the whole church and all who heard about these events" (Acts 5:11).

This incident acted to purify the Church and to warn the people by the gift of the Word of Knowledge that sin could not be concealed from a holy God. "You may be sure your sin will find you out" (Numbers 32:23).

Keep in mind, however, that there are no mind readers in the Church. This we need not fear. The Lord does not generally deal with our private and personal sins in this manner. He does deal harshly with sins against Himself and His holiness, however.

The Word of Knowledge is a gift. It is revelational in nature. By it hidden acts and motivations of a sinful nature are revealed and brought to light. The Spirit reveals conditions that otherwise could not be known naturally.

Again, this is a gift. God gives the gifts as He will. A gift such as this carries a great and grave responsibility for those who possess it. One should desire spiritual gifts and be pleased with the gifts the Lord gives him. Paul said, "Since you are eager to have spiritual gifts, try to excel in gifts that build up the church" (I Corinthians 14:12).

All God's people are gifted people. All the gifts are needed to guide, edify and purify the Church. Each believer should seek to discover his/her gifts and then willingly serve in that capacity.

QUESTION 39: Is it scriptural to lay on hands for the reception of the Spirit?

ANSWER: Yes it is. There are two ways God gives His Holy Spirit today. One is by a sovereign act when God simply pours out His Spirit with no human involvement. This is seen in Acts 2 and 10. The second way is demonstrated in Acts 8 and 19 when the apostles laid on hands for the reception of the Spirit. Both ways are correct and proper.

In our activities thus far, God has honored this ministry with nearly 20,000 men and women, boys and girls manifesting the baptism with the Spirit. They spoke in tongues at the time. We laid hands on the majority of them, but many manifested the gift by a sovereign act of God, some as they sat in the pews. Both ways are beautiful and we are pleased with the method God chooses for each occasion.

Can anyone lay on hands for the reception of the Spirit? This is a good question. The Scriptures seem to designate the laying on of hands for the impartation of the Spirit to be an apostolic gift (Acts 8). Some men and women are particularly gifted in this respect.

However, it is surely proper for believers to assemble in prayer and pray with one another and lay on hands, for God answers the prayers of His people. We have seen folk manifest the Spirit in these groups. We encourage it. God uses us all.

QUESTION 40: It seems that every time you pray with someone, he easily manifests the Holy Spirit by speaking with tongues. Is this true in all your meetings? Have there been occasions in which some did not receive? If not, why not? How do you help them?

ANSWER: This is generally true. All who desire to manifest the Spirit in our seminars do so easily and readily at our invitation. We teach them the practical simplicity of receiving and accepting the gift. We teach that all believers receive the Spirit at the time of salvation (Romans 8:9 and I Corinthians 6:19). They only await the outward manifestation, which is speaking in tongues. When a person grasps this thought, he can more freely yield himself to the Spirit.

There have been times when certain individuals did not manifest, usually due to personal inhibitions, fears or self-consciousness. Incorrect teaching in the past or wrong expectations may also hinder a person from freely letting go and getting in the flow.

If they do not receive in the public meeting, we do not embarrass them. Rather, we instruct them that they do indeed have the Spirit, and since we have laid hands on them, they are to go home and seek the Lord in their privacy and just let it happen. This works out fine. We have received testimonies to this effect. We believe that the things of God ought to be simple enough so that the 'least' child of God should be able to enter in and receive the blessing.

QUESTION 41: Many Christians in leadership positions in the non-Pentecostal churches show evidence in their daily lives that they are filled with the Spirit, but they do not speak with tongues. We know people who practice tongues on a regular basis whose lives do not demonstrate that they are filled with the Spirit. Why is this?

ANSWER: We point out that the gift of the Holy Spirit is just that, a gift. God does not give His gifts to only good and perfect people, for then none would qualify. God is not a respecter of persons (see Matthew 5:45). Really, "There is none good but one, that is God," said Jesus in Matthew 19:17.

Again, we should not compare the conduct of the non-tongues speakers with that of the tongues-speakers. This can be unfair. There are examples of good and bad conduct on both sides. Also, since devotional tongues are a manifestation, it is not a sign of spirituality. The fruit of the Spirit is in the lives of believers, whether they speak with tongues or not. It is the sign that one is filled [controlled] by the Spirit. The matter of spiritual control is the underlying theme here. "Thus, by their fruit will you recognize them" (Matthew 7:20).

This question is not an argument for or against tongues. We must follow the objective Word of God to ascertain its doctrinal teachings. However, Christians who speak with tongues should strive to be the finest examples of Spirit-filled believers anywhere.

QUESTION 42: Is there an artificial or counterfeit tongues experience? Are there some tongues that tongues-speakers experience that are not the real thing?

ANSWER: We do not believe, nor accept as a possibility, that there is an artificial or counterfeit tongues experience relative to the reception of the baptism with the Holy Spirit.

In the past when believers sought for the filling of the Holy Spirit in the Pentecostal churches, many of them did not understand the operation of the Spirit. The outpouring of the Spirit around the turn of the century was too new. God was doing a new thing in our day.

In the attempt to guard the purity of doctrinal experience, on occasion some made remarks in the prayer meetings to the seekers such as, "Be careful, you might get a wrong thing" (i.e., a wrong experience). "Be sure it is a clear language." "It might be gibberish," or "Satan talks in tongues, too, you know."

These kinds of statements from scripturally unlearned people have frightened and instilled suspicion in many of those who seek the manifestation of the Spirit. They became fearful lest they offend God by speaking on their own initiative, or thinking that they may possibly pre-empt the Spirit. These kinds of remarks have produced an unhealthy fear of the heavenly Father who "gives good gifts to them that ask Him" (Luke 11:13). Some people have developed guilt complexes from these tragic episodes and stopped seeking the Spirit altogether.

We now know differently, however. In His parables of the Fatherhood of God (Luke 11:11-13), Jesus said,

> Which of you fathers, if your son asks for a fish, will give him a snake instead? Or if he asks for an egg, will give him a scorpion? If you then, though you are evil, know how to give good gifts to your children, how much more will your father in heaven give the Holy Spirit to those who ask him?

It follows then that when we ask to manifest the Holy Spirit, that is exactly what we will do. To assert otherwise is to accuse God the Father of duplicity or deception. It seems to me that this borders on blasphemy. But God is gracious, for these mistaken statements have been said in ignorance. Some have invited people to their churches to experience the Spirit, and then frightened them out of the church with these scare tactics.

Let us be clear. There are from 7,000 to 10,000 languages and dialects in the world today. Any of these languages could be spoken when a person speaks with tongues—tongues that are not learned by the speaker. Some of these languages sound like grunts and groans, not distinguishable to the untrained ear. However, we must not call any of them 'unclear,' or 'gibberish,' simply because we do not understand them. Those tongues [languages] are perfectly clear to the people who learn them as their native tongue. They have no difficulty understanding each other. Paul said, "Undoubtedly there are all sorts of languages in the world, yet none of them is without meaning" (I Corinthians 14:10).

We believe that when anyone speaks with tongues, it is the 'real thing,' and that unless the hearer knows the language being spoken, he is in no position to judge or evaluate it. The person seeking the manifestation of the Holy Spirit can and should feel perfectly free to 'enter-in' and manifest the Spirit (speak in tongues) at will.

QUESTION 43: Where in the world did some churches come up with the doctrine that tongues are of the devil?

ANSWER: When the Spirit of God begins to move in a people or a church in revival, or in answer to prayer for spiritual growth, unusual physical manifestations or demonstrations may occur. This has happened in most revival movements throughout history. During revivals great emotionalism may break forth with the gifts of the Spirit in evidence, speaking with tongues, miracles, healings, etc. This is a recurrent pattern of the Church and need not be feared.

At the same time, however, there are unspiritual (non-spiritual) people in the churches who do not want the supernatural with its attending manifestations. These people appear to be in the majority, it seems.

So in the attempt to squelch anything spiritual, the easiest way is to attribute it to the devil. The Pharisees did this in Jesus' day. Some have done this with tongues today. Well-known television preachers have made statements to this effect and it is curious that some closest in doctrine to the Pentecostals have held views such as these.

One young lady had become seriously ill in our community. She was a member of a leading Evangelical church, which did not believe in healing. Another pastor and I invited her to attend a healing meeting sponsored by the Assemblies of God. She attended and responded to the evangelist's call for prayer. Hands were laid on her and prayer was offered for her healing. She was instantaneously healed.

She returned to her church to testify to her healing, which was visible, but her church refused to hear her. She was told not to mention it to other church members because it was not their doctrine. Some felt that it was actually of the devil. Consequently, she and her husband left that church, received the manifestation of the Holy Spirit and become leaders in a fine Pentecostal church.

The noted missionary, Bruce Olson, had a similar experience when he met Jesus personally. His mainline church accused him of trying to be 'super spiritual' and better than everyone else. They felt he was misled.[72]

Also, some folks are afraid of fanaticism. After revival fires burn down, most emotionalism subsides with it. This is a normal thing. Dr. L. E. Maxwell, the founder of Prairie Bible Institute in Three Hills, Alberta, Canada, said in a public lecture, "My prayer is, 'Lord, give us revival without fanaticism. But, if you can't do that, give us revival anyway!'" I say "Amen" to that.

There will always be a battle between the spiritual and non-spiritual elements of the Church until Jesus comes and sets things right.

"Even so, Come Lord Jesus" (Revelation 20:20 KJV).

QUESTION 44: Why do some people use I Corinthians 13:8 to excuse themselves from the baptism with the Holy Spirit?

ANSWER: This is due to a misunderstanding of the Scriptures and the doctrine of the Holy Spirit and His gifts. The theme of I Corinthians 13 is Love. Chapter 12 delineates the gifts of the Spirit, and chapter 14 gives the rules and regulations for the operations of tongues, interpretation of tongues and prophecy in the assembly.

Paul's concern is that the gifts of the Spirit be demonstrated in the arena of love for the edification of the Church. Some folk were displaying their gifts in a show-like manner to bring recognition to themselves, as if they were spiritually superior to others.

Paul says, "Love never fails. But where there are prophecies, they will cease; where there are tongues, they will be stilled; where there is knowledge, it will pass away." Prophecy, tongues and knowledge are all gifts of the Spirit. True, they shall cease when "that which is perfect is come..." That which is perfect is the Lord Jesus Christ. They shall all cease at the same time.

We know that neither prophecy nor knowledge has passed away. Therefore we cannot say that tongues has ceased, particularly when we see the Pentecostal/Charismatic people now numbering over 500 million worldwide and are growing at the rate of 19 million per year. Let's enjoy all the gifts while we are in the Holy Spirit Age, or dispensation.

QUESTION 45: Can we pray in tongues as a means of spiritual warfare?

ANSWER: Yes, we can. This is possibly the greatest weapon in the arsenal of spiritual warfare. Paul said, "Pray in the Spirit [tongues] on all occasions with all kinds of prayers and requests" (Ephesians 6:18). Jude said, "But you, dear friends, build yourselves up in your most holy faith and pray in the Holy Spirit" (v. 20).

These Scriptures teach us that we can come to God on any and every occasion and pray in the Spirit. Also, we can keep ourselves in God's love by doing so. In fact, both Ephesians 6:18 and Jude 20 are given as commands in the Greek text. We are commanded to pray in the Spirit, and we are commanded to keep ourselves in the love of God.

It follows, then, that if believers prayed in the Spirit on a continual basis privately and corporately, they could maintain greater spirituality in the Church and keep the victory in their own souls. This is the key to victory in spiritual warfare. We see then the necessity if having been baptized with the Holy Spirit, to enable a person to pray in this manner.

QUESTION 46: Will a person who gives messages in tongues also eventually be able to interpret his own messages?

ANSWER: Yes, it is scriptural that he be prepared to do so. Scripture shows that the two gifts, tongues and interpretation of tongues, go hand-in-hand. The Bible reads in I Corinthians 14:13: "For this reason the man who speaks in a tongue should pray that he may interpret what he says."

If this injunction were carefully observed and carried out, we would always be edified when a message was given to the church. When a message in tongues comes forth and no one interprets (as happens on occasion), the church is not blessed, and the unbeliever is not helped (I Corinthians 14:23-25). When a person speaks in tongues in the church, he should be prepared to interpret his own message in the event that no one else does.

QUESTION 47: Is it possible to discern whether a person who is speaking in tongues is in the flesh or in the Spirit?

ANSWER: I am uncomfortable trying to make this distinction. I do not think it is a matter of 'flesh' or 'spirit.' Perhaps it is rather a matter of timing.

A Spirit-baptized person can speak in tongues at will. It is volitional. I Corinthians 14:32 addresses this principle. In any case it would be his spirit that prays (v. 14). When one speaks in tongues in the assembly, he should be taught how the Spirit leads, how he can best fit in with the worship service, and be a blessing to the church.

His speaking should not interfere with the order of worship nor should it interfere with the preaching of the Word. From our observation the gifts of the Spirit are manifested to the greatest advantage during or immediately following the worship service.

This is most likely a matter of spiritual education. Let us not be too hasty to say that someone is 'in the flesh' lest we become judges of our brethren, and discourage them from participating in the gifts altogether. On the contrary there is the possibility that we may not be 'prayed up' ourselves, or in a spiritual state of mind to enjoy the gifts on an occasion.

QUESTION 48: Is it Scriptural to have prayer for a refilling of the Holy Spirit? Sometimes I get so dry.

ANSWER: Yes, of course. We need all the prayer we can get. In the book of Acts (2:4 and 4:31) we read the accounts where the saints were refilled (refueled). In Ephesians Paul said, "...be filled with the Spirit. Speak to one another with psalms and hymns and spiritual songs. Sing and make melody in your heart to the Lord" (5:18). He literally said, "Be *being* filled with the Spirit..." (italics mine). This filling is meant to be a continuous experience. To be filled with the Spirit is a command.

We need a good spiritual charge or anointing for each task we undertake. So pray all you can. Get involved in as many prayer meetings as possible. We need to heed the admonition the writer penned to the Hebrews:

> Let us not give up meeting together, as some are in the habit of doing, but let us encourage one another—and all the more as you see the Day approaching (Hebrews 10:25).

We need a reserve, a reservoir, so to speak, of spiritual energy to carry us over the spiritually dry times that come into our lives.

QUESTION 49: Is 'dancing in the spirit' scriptural? If it is scriptural, what is it?

ANSWER: Both of these are good questions. We believe dancing in the spirit is scriptural, if only by implication and example. We know of no biblical teachings or commands to do so, however. The term, 'dancing in the spirit,' is not used in the Scriptures, but on occasion someone "danced before the Lord."

Perhaps the best example is that of King David when he brought the Ark of the Covenant back to Jerusalem (II Samuel 6). He was "leaping and dancing before the Lord" (v. 16). Nowhere was he told to do this, but he did so in response to the joy and exultation he felt toward God. David said that it was "before the Lord" that he had done this.

There are numerous incidents where this has happened in revival meetings in which joy and enthusiasm were manifested in a great emotional response to the moving of the Spirit. The Psalmist said, "You turned my wailing (weeping) into dancing" (30:11). This is not likely a rehearsed routine of a particular dance step. Rather, a free physical motion of light stepping, skipping, leaping about and jumping, a time of uninhibited, expressive joy and merriment—which the Lord delights in.

People around the world do these things when they are jubilant. It is a physical, bodily expression of joyous emotion. These are not to be despised. Neither are they to be rejected out of hand. God knows that we need more joy than some of us seem to have. Let us feel free to express it in glorifying God.

Miriam, Moses' sister, danced before the Lord (Exodus 15:20), as did Jephthah's daughter (Judges 11:34). The Psalmist said, "Let them praise his name with dancing and make music to him with tambourine and harp" (149:3). "Praise him with tambourine and dancing" (150:4). We can free our emotions to rejoice in God our Savior. We therefore welcome clapping the hands, stomping the feet and dancing before the Lord.

Some congregations of worship teams practice or rehearse dancing in the Spirit. Others perform choreographed and worship routines. There are no biblical examples or statements regarding the use of these methods. Many consider them to be valid anyway and feel they add a beautiful dimension to the worship experience. Others do not have an appreciation for these art forms, and prefer that they not be included in their worship services. "Let everyone be fully persuaded in his own mind" may be a good admonition here.

QUESTION 50: What does it mean to be 'slain in the Spirit?'

ANSWER: The term 'slain in the Spirit' takes its name from the act in which a person falls to the floor in a religious meeting, generally under emotional impact. Often it occurs when hands are laid on in prayer. The term 'slain in the Spirit' is not found in the Scriptures, however.

We have seen this phenomenon on numerous occasions. I prayed for a lady for healing who had been diagnosed with a severe case of heart trouble. I laid hands on her and she immediately fell to the floor and lay there for fifteen to twenty minutes. We let her lie there while we prayed for others. After a little time she arose and exclaimed, "I'm healed!"

I replied, "If you are healed, go to your doctor and let him tell you so." She did just that. In a few days she returned to testify to the church that she was healed. God was glorified and the saints edified.

We have seen this on a grander scale in larger meetings. It is a fairly common thing among many of the Pentecostals. We know of no commands in this regard. We do not seek it nor do we foster it in our meetings. But when it does happen, we understand it and do not hinder it.

The late Reverend Lorne Fox at one time had one of the greatest healing ministries in the nation. Nearly everyone he prayed for was instantaneously healed. They fell to the floor like dead people, even before he touched them. He called it "God's operating table." Today you can see spectacular episodes of it in Benny Hinn's meetings, for example. God's ways are beyond our comprehension and knowledge.

QUESTION 51: After receiving the manifestation of the Spirit, is it scriptural for a person to receive a special filling to empower him for a specific ministry?

ANSWER: Yes. In Acts 2 believers received the baptism with the Holy Spirit and manifested it in speaking in tongues. This appears to be the normative manifestation of the Spirit in the New Testament. In Acts 4:31 they were filled again for service while under severe persecution. "And they were all filled with the Holy Spirit and spoke the word of God boldly." They offered a special prayer for the occasion.

There was the laying on of hands for the ministry gifts in the New Testament. Paul told Timothy, "Do not neglect your gift, which was given you through a prophetic message when the body of elders laid their hands on you" (I Timothy 4:14). He then stated it more positively: "For this reason I remind you to fan into flame the gift of God, which is in you through the laying on of my hands" (II Timothy 1:6). Jesus said in Acts 1:8, "You will receive power when the Holy "Spirit comes on you..." This can be translated to read "whenever the Spirit comes upon you," or "every time the Spirit comes upon you."

Also, hands were laid on the seven men who were chosen to be deacons to serve tables in Acts 6. They were already filled with the Spirit. It is scriptural for one to receive a special filling or anointing for a specific ministry.

QUESTION 52: I have been filled with the Spirit a short time, and sometimes when I pray, I wonder if I am really speaking in tongues, or making up the words myself. Am I speaking a language, or just a bunch of sounds I put together? How do I now if it is really my prayer language? Also, could this be the devil trying to discourage me?

ANSWER: Yours is not an unusual question to

consider. Too many of God's people feel that God should 'take over' their entire being and cause them to speak in tongues while they remain passive. This is not the way it usually is.

We teach that a person receives (takes) the Holy Spirit by faith. The problem seems to be that we have so little faith at times. We want God to do it *all*. But He invites man's cooperation. This is usually the way it is. Why do we have difficulty accepting the fact that God almighty desires our cooperation? If God were to do it all, no faith would be required on our part.

A concomitant question is, when a person speaks in tongues, is it the 'person,' or is it 'God' who speaks? The answer is, it is both the person and God who speak in a cooperative effort. By faith we open our mouths, use our voices, sounds, breath and lips and speak out. This is a volitional act we enter into by faith in the spiritual transaction with God.

We have the responsibility to speak out. God is responsible for what is spoken. We move first in faith (speaking) and God moves in answer by supplying the words we speak in tongues. This may or may not be an emotional experience at the moment. Emotions will come in time if we are patient.

This being so, we are not in a position to judge or evaluate the tongues spoken. Most of us are not linguists. As I have pointed out, there are approximately 7,000 to 10,000 languages and dialects in the world today. By faith we accept our tongue or language as being one of them and we put it into practice.

I know it is really my prayer language because it is not my natural language and I did not do this until I was baptized in the Spirit. The beauty of it is that I have the ability to cooperate and work with God in the things of the Spirit. This increases my faith in God and a desire for more of God. Do not try to evaluate your prayer language too quickly. Wait for a year or so and see what it has done for you.

Perhaps Satan would try to discourage you. Why would he want to do this? The prayer language is an effective tool in your spiritual warfare. It is a weapon you may use against the 'wiles of the Enemy.' It is powerful. However, doubts come about due to our lack of faith or misunderstanding of the working of God's Spirit. Keep practicing your prayer language by faith until it becomes second nature with you, that is, spiritually natural.

QUESTION 53: Paul said in I Corinthians 12:31 that we are to seek the greater gifts. What are they?

ANSWER: In I Corinthians 12 Paul lists nine gifts of the Spirit. In Romans 12 and Ephesians 4 he lists others. In these passages the Apostle does not rank the gifts. In fact, they overlap. Therefore no importance relative to a particular gift is suggested. So we can say that there are no 'greater' gifts per se. Each gift is equally important in its place, time and function. The text should read as a simple indicative statement, not an imperative as most English versions seem to suggest. The Greek form of the verb is the same for each case, the indicative and the imperative. Context decides the usage.

As I mentioned, the Corinthians were eager to show off the manifestation of tongues to the neglect of the other gifts. They believed that this display signified spirituality. The Apostle wished to correct this fallacy. He asked rhetorically, "Are all apostles? Are all prophets? Are all teachers? Do all work miracles? Do all have the gifts of healing? (The implied answer to all of these is, "No.") But you are eagerly desiring the greater [flamboyant] gifts."[73] Paul uses "greater" in the sense of being flashier, or a show-off. The footnote continues, "The Corinthians were apparently seeking status through the exercise of the gifts that seemed to them to be more important."

The New Testament Scholar Gordon D. Fee addressed this issue when he translated the passage as: "But you are seeking the *so-called* greater gifts" (Italics mine).[74] In reality there are no greater gifts. All are equally important in their place and function.

References

Allinder, Myrl. "Power," *VOICE*. Los Angeles: Full Gospel Business Men's Fellowship, International. July-August, 1971.

Acts, The Communicator's Commentary. Lloyd J. Ogilvie, Ed. Waco: Word Books, 1983. Vol. 5.

Analytical Greek Lexicon Revised. (1978 Edition). Harold K. Moulton, Ed. Grand Rapids: Zondervan, 1978.

Anchor Bible. Vol. 31. Garden City, NY: Doubleday & Company, Inc., 1967.

Ashcroft, J. Robert. *The Sequence of the Supernatural*. Springfield, MO: Gospel Publishing House, 1972.

Auch, Ron. *Pentecostals in Crisis*. Green Forest, AR: New Leaf Press, 1988.

Barclay, William. *New Testament Words*. London: SCM Press, Ltd., 1964.

Basham, Don. *Spiritual Power*. Springdale, PA: Whitaker House, 1971.

Bennett, Dennis and Riga. *The Holy Spirit and You*. Plainfield, NJ: Logos, 1971.

Bittlinger, Arnold. *Gifts and Graces*. Grand Rapids: Wm. B. Eerdmans Publishing Company, 1967.

Bredesen, Harold. "Empowered by the Supernatural." *CHARISMA*. Lake Mary, FL: Strang Publications, August 1994.

Bresson, Bernard L. *Studies in Ecstasy*. New York: Vantage Press, 1996.

Bruce, F. F. *The Book of Acts. New Testament Commentary on the New Testament*. Grand Rapids: Wm. B. Eerdmans Publishing Company, 1955.

Brumback, Carl. *What Meaneth This?* Springfield, MO: Gospel Publishing House, 1947.

Campolo, Tony. *The Kingdom of God is a Party*. Dallas, Word Publishing, 1990.

Cantelon, Willard. *The Baptism of the Holy Spirit*. Plainfield, MO: Logos, 1971.

Carothers, Merlin R. *Prison to Praise*. Lake Mary, FL: Strang Publications, 1970.

Cho, Paul Yonggi. *The Holy Spirit, My Senior Partner*. Altamonte Springs, FL: Creation House, 1989.

Cox, Don. *Tongues: A to Z*. Iowa: Author, 1972.

Christenson, Laurence. *Speaking in Tongues*. Minneapolis: Bethany Fellowship Publishers, 1968.

Clarke's Commentary. Nashville: Abingdon-Cokesbury Press. Vol. 1, 5.

Crabtree, Charles T. *The Pentecostal Priority*, Springfield MO: Decade of Harvest, 1993.

Dunn, James D. G. *Baptism in the Holy Spirit*. Philadelphia: Westminster Press, 1970.

Du Plessis, David. *The Spirit Bade Me Go*. Plainfield, NJ: Logos, 1970.

Expositor's Bible Commentary. Frank Gaebelein, Ed. Grand Rapids: Zondervan House Publisher, 1979.

Farah, Charles. *VIEW*. Costa Mesa, CA: Full Gospel Businessmen's Fellowship, International, 1966. No. 13.

Fee, Gordon D. *The First Epistle to the Corinthians. The New International Commentary on the New Testament* (NICNT). Grand Rapids: William B. Eerdmans Publishing Company, 1987.

References

Frodsham, Stanley Howard. *Smith Wigglesworth, Apostle of Faith*. Springfield, MO: Gospel Publishing House, 1973.
_____. *The Spirit-Filled LIFE*. Grand Rapids: Wm. B. Eerdmans Publishing Company, 1936.
Frost, Robert C. *Aglow with the Spirit*. Plainfield, NJ: Logos, 1965.
Gee, Donald. *God's Grace and Power for Today*. Springfield, MO: Gospel Publishing House, 1936.
Olson, Bruce. *Bruchko*. Lake Mary, FL: Creation House, Strang Publications, 1995.
Pache, Rene. *The Person and Work of the Holy Spirit*. Chicago: Moody Press, 1954.
Palma, Anthony D. "Another Look at Acts 2:4." *ADVANCE*. Springfield, MO: Gospel Publishing House, September, 1994.
_____. *The Spirit—God in Action*. Springfield, MO: Gospel Publishing House, 1974.
Pink, Arthur W. *The Holy Spirit*. Grand Rapids. Baker Book House, 1970.
Religious News Service: Orange County Register. Orange County, California. July 20, 1991.
Roberts, Oral. *The Holy Spirit in the Now*. (Tape Series) Tulsa, OK: Oral Roberts University.
Sheets, Dutch. *Intercessory Prayer*. Ventura, CA: Regal Books, 1996.
Sherrill, John L. *They Speak with Other Tongues*. Old Tappan, NJ: Spire Books, 1964.
Shoemaker, Samuel M. *With the Holy Spirit and Fire*. Waco: Word Books. 1960.
Spitler, Russell, *The Corinthian Correspondence*. Springfield, MO: Gospel Publishing House, 1976.
Stern, David H. *Jewish New Testament Commentary*. Clarksville, MD: Jewish New Testament Publications, 1992.

Stiles, J. E. *The Gift of the Holy Spirit.* P.O. Box 3174, Burbank, CA. 91504.

Stott, John R. W. *The Baptism and Fullness of the Holy Spirit.* Downer's Grove, IL: InterVarsity Press, 1964.

Synan, Vinson. *The Twentieth-Century Pentecostal Explosion.* Altamonte Springs, FL: Creation House, 1987.

The Communicator's Commentary. Lloyd J. Ogilvie, Ed. Waco: Word Books, 1987. Vol. 1.

The Expositor's Bible Commentary. Frank E. Gaebelein, Ed. Grand Rapids: Zondervan Publishing House, 1981. Vol. 9.

The Expositor's Greek Testament. W. Robertson Nicoli, Ed. Grand Rapids: Wm. B. Eerdmans Publishing Company. Vol. II, p. 217.

The Witness. Lay Witness for Christ, International. October, 1991.

Torrey, R. A. *What the Bible Teaches.* Grand Rapids: Fleming H. Revell, 1993.

Tournier, Paul. *The Meaning of Persons.* NY: Harper and Row Publishers, 1957.

Trueblood, Elton. *The Company of the Committed.* NY: Harper and Row Publishers, 1962.

Tyndale New Testament Commentaries. Grand Rapids: Wm. B. Eerdmans Publishing Company, 1959. Vol. 5.

Vidler, Alec R. *Christian Belief.* London: SCM Press, 1950.

VOICE. Los Angeles, CA: Full Gospel Business Men's Fellowship, International. July-August 1971.

Wagner, C. Peter. *Your Spiritual Gifts.* Ventura, CA: Regal Books, 1982.

Wigglesworth, Smith. *On the Holy Spirit.* New Kensington, PA: Whitaker House, 1998.

Williams, J. Rodman. *The Pentecostal Reality.* Plainfield, NJ: Logos, 1972.

References

_____. *The Era of the Spirit*. Plainfield, NJ: Logos, 1971.

Womack, David A. *Pentecostal Experience: The Writings of Donald Gee*. Springfield, MO: Gospel Publishing House, 1993.

_____. *ReAction News Letter*. ACTS IN ACTION, Green Valley, AZ. Summer 2001.

_____. *The Wellsprings of the Pentecostal Movement*. Springfield, MO: Gospel Publishing House, 1968.

World Christian Encyclopedia. David B. Barrett, Ed. New York: Oxford University Press. 1982.

Index

[1] *Acts, The Communicator's Commentary.* Lloyd J. Ogilvie, (Ed.) Waco: Word Books, Publisher, 1983. Vol. 5.

[2] Judges 13:6; I Kings 18:30-40; II Kings 2:115: cf. Numbers 11:26-29.

[3] Hebrews 8:6-10.

[4] See Romans 7.

[5] F. F. Bruce, *The Book of Acts.* The New International Commentary on the New Testament, p. 72.

[6] Ibid.

[7] Paul Tournier, *The Meaning of Persons.* New York, NY: Harper & Row, 1957, pp. 172-173.

[8] *Clarke's Commentary,* Vol. 1, p. 352.

[9] Tournier, op. cit.

[10] *Tyndale New Testament Commentary,* Vol. 5, p. 58.

[11] *Clarke's Commentary,* Vol. 5, p. 696.

[12] *Interpreter's Bible.* Vol. 9, p. 43.

[13] Tyndale, op. cit.

[14] *Expositor's Bible Commentary.* Frank Gaebelein, (Ed.) Grand Rapids: Zondervan House Publisher. 1979, vol. 9, p. 253.

[15] Ibid.

[16] Hebrews 9:23ff.

[17] *ISBE.* Geoffrey W. Bromiley, (Ed.) Grand Rapids: William B. Eerdmans Publishing House, 1979, vol. 1, p. 362.

[18] David A. Womack, *Pentecostal Experience: The Writings of Donald Gee.* Springfield, MO: The Gospel Publishing House, 1993. p. 98.

[19] Anchor Bible. Johannes Munck, *The Acts of the Apostles*. Garden City, NY: Doubleday & Company, Inc. 1967, Vol. 31, p. 13.

[20] See John R. W. Stott. *The Baptism and Fullness of the Holy Spirit*. Downer's Grove, IL: InterVarsity Press, 1964, pp. 19-23.

[21] See James G. D. Dunn, *Baptism in the Holy Spirit*. Philadelphia: Westminster Press. 1979.

[22] Stott. Op. cit.

[23] G. Campbell Morgan, *The Acts of the Apostles*, Fleming H. Revell Company. Old Tappan, New Jersey: 1924.

[24] For further study, see *Tyndale New Testament Commentary*, Vol. 5, pp. 155-156; *Acts, Communicator's Commentary*, Vol. 5, p. 273.

[25] Carl Brumback, *What Meaneth This?* Springfield, MO: Gospel Publishing House, 1947, pp. 208-214.

[26] The Analytical Greek Lexicon Revised, p. 88.

[27] Expositor's Greek Testament, Vol. 2, p. 217.

[28] *NIV New Study Bible*, Acts 8:16 Note.

[29] Brumback, p. 276. Brumback notes that God has prescribed standards for each generation in which men are to be judged. Those standards do not change or fluctuate. But with mankind He appears to have permitted changes and settled for less. He has had to suspend judgment at times due to people's inability to conform to His standards. He may even bear with His people now in that the many are not spiritually inclined to be filled with the Spirit and follow Him implicitly in believing and obeying Scripture.

[30] Myrl Allinder, "Power," *VOICE*. Los Angeles: Full Gospel Business Men's Fellowship, International, July-August, 1971.

[31] See *NIV Study Bible* notes on Mark 16:9-20.

[32] Arnold Bittlinger, *Gifts and Graces*. Grand Rapids: William. B. Eerdmans Publishing Company, 1967, p. 102.

[33] Quoted in Bittlinger, *Op. Cit.*, p. 102.

[34] Morton T. Kelsey, *Tongue Speaking*. New York: Doubleday & Company, 1968, p. 100.

[35] Quoted in Bittlinger, *Op. Cit.*, p. 102

[36] Paul Tournier, *The Meaning of Persons*, New York: Harper and Row, 1957, p. 172, 173.

[37] Bittlinger, *Op. Cit.,* p. 102.

[38] Dutch Sheets, *Intercessory Prayer*. Ventura, California: Regal Books, 1996, p. 100.

[39] *Tyndale New Testament Commentaries*. Grand Rapids: William. B. Eerdmans Publishing Company, 1959. Vol. 18, p. 184.

Index

[40] Mings, Sam. "The Mings Dynasty: How could it Fall?" *VOICE.* Summer, 1991.

[41] "The Witness." *Lay Witnesses for Christ International.* October 1991.

[42] R. A. Torrey, *What the Bible Teaches.* Old Tappan, NJ: Fleming H. Revell Company, 1933, p. 270.

[43] Arnold Bittlinger, *Gifts and Graces.* Grand Rapids: Wm. B. Eerdmans Publishing Company, 1967, p. 101.

[44] Ibid.

[45] NIV Study Bible, p. 1753 (note).

[46] Paul Tournier, *The Meaning of Persons.* New York: Harper and Row, 1957, pp. 172-173.

[47] *Charisma*, February 1982.

[48] *Orange County Register*, July 20, 1991.

[49] Alec R. Vidler, *Christian Belief.* London: SCM Press, 1950, p. 59.

[50] G. Campbell Morgan. *The Birth of the Church.* Old Tappan, NJ: Fleming Revell Company, 1968, p. 39.

[51] Cf. *Interpreter's Bible.* Vol. 9, p. 43.

[52] Tony Campolo, *The Kingdom of God is a Party.* Dallas: Word Publishing, 1990, p. 28.

[53] *ISBE.* Vol. 3, p. 757.

[54] *ISBE.* Vol. 2, p. 293.

[55] G. Campbell Morgan, *The Acts of the Apostles.* Old Tappan, NJ: Fleming Revell Company, 1924, p. 29.

[56] Walter J. Hollenweger, *The Pentecostals.* Minneapolis: Augsburg Publishing House, 1972, p. 114.

[57] *Ibid*, p. 335.

[58] *Ibid.*

[59] *Ibid.*

[60] Charles Farah, *VIEW*, No. 1. Full Gospel Businessmen's Fellowship, International, p. 9.

[61] Comments made in private instruction in the United States Naval Chaplains School, Newport, Rhode Island, 1963.

[62] *The Twentieth Century New Testament.*

[63] I Corinthians 14:2. Phillips Translation, *Letters to Young Churches.*

[64] Don Basham, *Spiritual Power.* Springdale, Pennsylvania: Whitaker House, 1971, pp. 47-49.

[65] David Womack, *Pentecostal Experience: The Writings of Donald Gee.* Springfield, MO: Gospel Publishing House, 1993, p. 23.

[66] Stanford E. Linzey, "The Evangelist and the Holy Spirit," *Evangelists Fellowship Newsletter*, Springfield, MO: Summer, 1991.

[67] Elton Trueblood, *The Company of the Committed*. NY: Harper & Row, Publishers. 1962, p. 56.

[68] Acts 2:4. *Moffatt New Testament*.

[69] C. Peter Wagner, *Your Spiritual Gifts*. Ventura, CA. Regal Books. 1982.

[70] David H. Stern, *Jewish New Testament Commentary*. Clarksville, MO: Jewish New Testament Publications, 1992, p. 212.

[71] See William Barclay, *New Testament Words*. London: SCM Press, Ltd. 1964, pp. 77-84.

[72] Bruce Olson, *Bruchko*, Lake Mary, Florida: Creation House, Strang Communications, 1995.

[73] I Corinthians 12:31, *NIV Study Bible Footnote*.

[74] The Epistle to the Corinthians, NICNT, p. 624.

Printed in the United States
44315LVS00003B/182